P9-CWE-664

The three cons stood before Bolan like a wall of malignant flesh...

Their hard thick bodies were tense and bristling, and crudely made blades shone dully in their hands.

Bolan eyeballed each man carefully, analyzing strengths and weaknesses from the way they moved. He didn't find many weaknesses.

Rodeo, the leader, chuckled. "You boys can cut him up some," he said. "But I want him alive." He lifted his studded knuckles. "For these."

The Executioner fell into his combat stance and looked down the narrow corridor.

There was no way out....

MACK BOLAN

The Executioner

DON PENDLETON's EXECUTIONER
MACK BOLAN

Savannah Swingsaw

A GOLD EAGLE BOOK FROM
W💥RLDWIDE

TORONTO • NEW YORK • LONDON • PARIS
AMSTERDAM • STOCKHOLM • HAMBURG
ATHENS • MILAN • TOKYO • SYDNEY

First edition February 1985

ISBN 0-373-61074-2

Special thanks and acknowledgment to
Ray Obstfeld for his contributions to this work.

Copyright © 1985 by Worldwide Library.
Philippine copyright 1985. Australian copyright 1985.

All rights reserved. Except for use in any review, the
reproduction or utilization of this work in whole or in part
in any form by any electronic, mechanical or other means,
now known or hereafter invented, including xerography,
photocopying and recording, or in any information storage
or retrieval system, is forbidden without the permission
of the publisher, Worldwide Library, 225 Duncan Mill Road,
Don Mills, Ontario, Canada M3B 3K9.

All the characters in this book have no existence outside the
imagination of the author and have no relation whatsoever to
anyone bearing the same name or names. They are not even
distantly inspired by any individual known or unknown to the
author, and all the incidents are pure invention.

The Worldwide Library trademarks consisting of the words
GOLD EAGLE and THE EXECUTIONER are registered
in the United States Patent Office and in the Canada Trade
Marks Office. The Gold Eagle design trademark, the Executioner
design trademark, the Mack Bolan design trademark, the globe
design trademark, and the Worldwide design trademark
consisting of the word WORLDWIDE in which the
letter "O" is represented by a depiction of a globe, are
trademarks of Worldwide Library.

Printed in Canada

Man, when perfected, is the best of animals, but when separated from law and justice, he is the worst of all.

—Aristotle

I often wonder how other people see Mack Bolan. Personally, I feel he's incorruptible, selfless and entirely committed. I don't think he necessarily likes what he's doing, but someone has to do it. And he's not bitter or cynical about this world. If all this personifies the perfect man, then so be it.

—Hal Brognola
Director of Sensitive Operations Group, Stony Man liaison with the Oval Office.

Dedicated to Sir Anthony Berry,
British cabinet minister
in Prime Minister Margaret Thatcher's government,
who died as a result of a terrorist bombing
at the Grand Hotel in Brighton, England, 1984.

1

The squad car chased Bolan into the dark alley. An unexpected flash thundershower an hour before had left the pavement slick and shiny under the full moon's harsh light. Bolan's feet splashed through muddy potholes as he ran, bumping overstuffed trash cans, spooking a prowling tomcat.

Behind him, the police cruiser followed slowly, relentlessly, colored lights pulsing atop the roof. Bolan could hear the worn shock absorbers squeak as the car bounced over the ruts in the road. The only way out of this alley now was straight ahead.

Another thirty yards of slimy wet hardtop would see him to the other end. If the cops decided they weren't in the mood to chase him, then a bullet would be faster, easier.... Well, he'd worry about that then.

Bolan raced for the end of the narrow street, a plain brown paper bag twisted at the neck and gripped in one hand, an untraceable Smith & Wesson Model 67 38 Combat Masterpiece in the other. He stuffed the sack into his worn leather aviator's jacket as he ran. The laneway opened onto Decatur Street, busy enough that he might get lost in the late evening weekend traffic.

In the distance, the headlights of passing cars and the moonlight lent a fluorescent effect to the scene. A dying man's fantasy of the pearly gates, Bolan thought with a grimace. The Executioner had no such fantasies. Not anymore. He'd seen enough of heaven and hell right here on earth.

"Stop!" The bullhorn from the squad car squawked. "Throw your gun down. *Now!*"

Bolan kept running, his arms and legs pistoning like a dragster's engine. Ten yards more. The humid Atlanta air slicked his skin, made his bulky clothes unbearable. He sucked in air hungrily, but the air was too hot to satisfy his burning lungs. Still, he headed for the open end of the alley.

Suddenly a second squad car bounced into view with squealing tires, plugging the exit. Its light whirled dizzily, its radio crackling with instructions from the dispatcher.

Bolan skidded to a stop as he saw the two uniformed men grab shotguns and spill onto the street. He spun and ran back the way he came, toward the first car.

The cruiser was also parked now, its doors open as far as they could go before scraping against a building. Behind each door crouched a young policeman, aiming a shotgun at Bolan.

"Drop it, hotshot," the black officer yelled from the driver's side. The young white cop behind the other door was blinking nervously. He looked as if he had a bad itch and the only way to scratch was to pull that trigger.

Bolan hesitated, glanced over his shoulder at the

two other cops kneeling behind their squad-car fenders.

Then something moved behind the trash can.

The white cop swung his shotgun around and squeezed off two rounds before his partner's crisp voice broke through the panic. "Jess! Damn it. Stop shooting!"

But the old dented garbage can already had a pair of fist-size holes chewed through it. The lid flew off and the can toppled over. The ragged metal edges scraped along the pavement as it tumbled lazily toward the second squad car, spilling garbage as it turned.

Behind where the can used to sit, a wet splotch of fur, blood and guts was all that was left of the cat. The fluids that had kept the small creature alive leaked out onto the damp ground, mixing with the oil, dirt and slime of a hundred other unwitnessed tragedies that had taken place in that dark alley.

"Hell, Jess," the black cop said, shaking his head. "You know better'n that. Now we gotta talk to a shooting team."

"Sorry, man," Jess said, shrugging.

The two cops at the other end were laughing. "Bagged yourself a real bobcat there, Jess," one of them taunted.

"Yessir," his partner joined in. "Meanest damn cat I ever seen. Fangs and claws and everything. Saved the whole damn city from certain destruction."

"Knock it off," the black cop shouted. Then he turned to Bolan, still frozen between the two squad cars' headlights. "Do yourself a favor, slick. Drop your gun and get down on your knees, hands on top of your head. Don't think about it, just do it."

Bolan tossed the .38 into a nearby puddle and folded his hands on his head.

"Fine, now on your knees."

"Don't push it," Bolan said quietly to him.

He didn't. The four cops stood up and closed in on the Executioner, their shotguns leveled at his chest.

"Get his gun, Jess," the black cop said.

The kid nodded, glanced over at the mangled lump of wet fur by the wall, swallowed something bitter in his throat, then bent over the muddy puddle and daintily fished out Bolan's .38 with two fingers.

One of the officers from the second squad car, the only one as big as Bolan, shoved him roughly up against the brick wall of the nearest building and frisked him. He pulled the paper bag out of Bolan's jacket and peered inside. "Hunnert and twenty-eight dollars. Same as was stolen from the liquor store."

"Wallet?" the black cop asked.

"Nope."

"Any ID?"

"Nuthin'. No car keys, parking stubs, not even chewing gum. Clean as duck spit."

The black officer clamped the cuffs on Bolan's wrists and used the shotgun to prod him toward the squad car. Jess dogged after them, still holding the dripping .38 between two fingers. "Meet you guys back at the station,'' the black cop told the other two.

They nodded, climbed back into their vehicle and backed it through the small crowd that had gathered at the mouth of the alley.

''Book him, Jess,'' the senior officer said, slamming the door behind Bolan.

2

Bolan sat at the gray metal table, wiping the ink from his fingertips with the rough paper towel. A skinny plainclothes policeman wearing an ill-fitting toupee sat across from him lazily moving a stir stick around in his Styrofoam cup of coffee. He hadn't offered Bolan any. In fact the only thing he offered Bolan was a chance to make one phone call.

They'd been sitting there for fifteen minutes, neither man speaking. The skinny cop just kept staring and stirring. The only sound was a faint rattling in the air-conditioning duct. If it wasn't for the rattle, Bolan wouldn't have known the air-conditioning was even on. The room must have been ninety-five degrees. The humidity was like an invisible gel pushing at him from all sides.

The skinny cop put down the cup and took off his jacket, all the time staring at Bolan. Dark wet stains drooped under each arm.

"Kinda hot in here for coffee," Bolan said.

"Is it hot in here?" the officer said.

That ended conversation for another ten minutes. The silent treatment was supposed to make Bolan nervous so he tried to act nervous, fidgeting with the inky paper towel, glancing anxiously at the clock on the wall, studying the green acoustic squares that paneled walls and ceiling.

Then the door opened and a scrappy-looking guy walked in, no taller than five foot six, but thick like a jeep. He wore a natty three-piece blue suit and carried a beat-up leather briefcase. Bolan guessed him to be around forty-two. "I got about two minutes, Culver. What we got here?" He had a soft Georgia accent.

"We got one smartass bad guy who won't give us his name."

"Mirandized?"

"Signed and sealed, Captain."

"Fingerprints?"

"Sent them in. They're checking now."

"Evidence?"

"Silent alarm from the liquor store. Boggs and Simpson caught him running away. Had a .38 and a bag from the liquor store with the exact amount of cash stolen. No ID on him."

"Witnesses?"

"We're bringing the liquor-store clerk down for a lineup. The clerk had been knocked on the head, but the wound's minor. There shouldn't be any problem. This guy fits the description perfectly."

The captain looked at Bolan. "You look like you been around the block before, sport. You gotta know that playing dummy won't get you nothing but hard time and pain."

"I'm saying nothing till I see my lawyer," Bolan said.

The captain shook his head. "Lock his ass up."

"Right." The skinny cop stood. "Notice those tiny scars around the eyes and nose, Captain?"

The captain squinted at Bolan's face. "You mean those wrinkles?"

"They're scars. My sister was in an accident when she was a kid. Her boyfriend had a snoot full and crashed his Studebaker into a tractor. Mashed her face something awful. Doctors did the best they could back then, but she never could breathe proper. Always chewing with her mouth open so's she could breathe. Ever watched yams chewed like that? Yeech."

"Get on with it, Jimmy."

The cop patted his toupee, shifting it. "Anyway, couple years ago she had it fixed and figured while they was at it they might as well do a little adjusting and tightening here and there. Had tiny threadlike scars just like this fella."

"What are you saying, Jimmy? This boy's had plastic surgery?"

"Looks that way."

The captain rubbed his chin. "Well, that don't change anything for now. Lock him up and wait for the fingerprint results. I think he's going to be spending some time in a Georgia jail."

There was a knock on the door.

The captain pulled it open. "What?"

The uniformed cop outside pointed to Bolan. "His lawyer's here. Wants to see him."

"In a second." The uniformed cop nodded and left. The captain faced the skinny plainclothes cop. "Let him jaw with his lawyer. Meantime, tell the

D.A. what we got. This looks like one case we won't have to bargain down. This tough guy's going all the way.''

3

"What kept you?" Bolan asked.

Hal Brognola closed the door behind him, dabbing at the sweat on his forehead with his handkerchief. "I see you've been busy making friends again. The precinct captain looked at me as if I were defending Charles Manson."

"I grow on people."

"The list of people you've grown on who want to yank your roots gets longer."

"That's why I'm here. Right?"

Brognola sighed as he sat down. "I'm not so sure this is such a good idea, Mack. You're leaving yourself wide open. It's still not too late to change your mind."

Bolan shook his head. "Appreciate the thought, Hal, but I'm already here. Things are moving according to plan. I should be out of here before the paperwork's even done. I don't think they'll make any connection between me and the Executioner. What about the liquor store clerk?"

"He'll pick you out of the lineup."

"His wounds?"

"The best makeup artist around applied them herself. Looks like you laid an eight-inch gash across his forehead. That should add another couple of years to your sentence.''

''Perfect.''

''Yeah, perfect,'' Brognola said wryly. He plucked a fat cigar from his pocket and roasted the end with a match. ''It's a bit hot for this,'' he explained, ''but it's the only way to kill the damn smell of this place.''

Bolan let his friend talk. He knew the man pretty well after all these years together. Recognized his discomfort at the situation. He'd seen Bolan hatch a lot of farfetched plans before, but this was the most bizarre of all. Or maybe just the most dangerous.

''What about the fingerprints?'' Bolan asked.

''Taken care of. It'll take them a day or two, but by then they'll match you through the FBI as Damon Blue. Your rap sheet would do any convict proud. Twelve arrests for armed robbery, assault, carrying a concealed weapon. Two convictions. Just like you wanted.''

''Good.''

Brognola blew a cloud of smoke at the ceiling. ''I'm glad you approve.''

''What about our target?''

''Dodge Reed is still locked up nice and snug at the county jail. No fights, no fuss. Model prisoner.''

''Any word on Zavlin?''

Brognola hesitated, his face suddenly grim. ''He's in the country.''

''Damn! Already?''

''Flew in last night from Soviet Union via Canada.

Lost our boys less than ten miles from Washington, D.C.''

Bolan grimaced. "He's their best. Maybe the best ever.''

And that's what started this whole charade, Bolan thought. Undercover sources in east Europe had passed word along the intelligence network that the KGB's best, most ruthless assassin had been assigned a new target for immediate elimination. Nothing unusual there.

Zavlin had been responsible for the assassinations of those bothersome to the KGB for years. When Zavlin was given a target's name, nothing could stop him. Many had tried.

The CIA routinely got advance notice on some of his marks and set up elaborate plans to foil the assassin. They never succeeded. Neither did the British, the Israelis nor any other government agency. All they ever got for their troubles was a long list of murdered field agents.

Many anti-Soviet leaders in Africa, South America and Europe had fallen under Zavlin's hand.

What was unusual about this case was Zavlin's current target: Dodge Reed. Brognola had run every kind of check on Reed that was possible and the profile always came out the same.

Dodge Reed was just what he appeared to be, a twenty-three-year-old record store employee who attended Atlanta Community College at night, lived alone in a one-bedroom apartment and drove a seven-year-old Pinto. Three weeks before he'd been arrested for embezzling from the record store he worked at. He was awaiting trial.

What would the KGB's best international hit man want with a guy like that?

"Nothing more on Reed?" Bolan asked. "No access to top-secret information?"

Brognola shook his head. "Nothing."

"Anything from your overseas agents?"

"Nope. Just that Reed is a top-priority kill. They want him dead within ninety-six hours."

"They know he's in jail?"

"They know."

Bolan frowned. "Damn! What does this kid know that scares them?"

"That's what you're here to find out." Brognola looked his old friend in the eye. "You know I wouldn't have come to you with this if there was any other way. Hell, you've got enough troubles of your own right now. It's just that we've finally got a chance to catch this monster and the usual agencies have failed too often. I don't want that to happen this time."

Bolan smiled. The words hadn't been necessary—not between them. "We'll get him," he said.

But even as he said the words, he wondered who'd get whom first.

4

The Executioner sat in the back of the squad car and stared through the wire-mesh screen at the nearby Blue Ridge Mountains. The sun was barely tinting Atlanta's skyline with pink. A slight breeze whipped through Atlanta today, but it was still hot. His prison garb was stiff and scratchy. The handcuffs, clamped on too tight by an overzealous guard, chafed at his wrists.

"Be on our way soon," the driver said, scratching at his uniform as if it was as starchy and hot as Bolan's.

They were idling inside the jail entrance while the driver's partner chatted with one of the gate guards. On the other side of the thick metal barrier, cars drifted slowly to work, to friends, to family, the occupants listening to their favorite deejay, planning their Sunday fun. Traffic was sparse, the city still sleepy.

They'd kept Bolan overnight at the precinct while the paperwork was shuffled from file folder to file cabinet. The fingerprints had finally been attached to a name and case history—Damon Blue. Their curiosity satisfied, the cops were anxious to kick him on to Fulton County Jail, where prisoners awaiting trial were held. Bolan knew that. Counted on it.

Because that's where Dodge Reed was.

And that's where Zavlin would have to kill him.

But why?

The reasons still baffled Bolan. The KGB's top eliminator coming halfway around the world to kill a nobody who was already locked up in prison. It didn't make sense. Yet.

It didn't matter. Whatever Bolan could do to sabotage the KGB was enough of an excuse. Taking out Zavlin in the process would just be icing on the cake.

"Can't figure you, son," the driver continued.

"What do you mean?" Bolan asked.

"I been a cop for close to twenty-eight years now. Pretty much tell the bad ones with just a glance. Don't matter what kind of clothes they wear or how much money they make or who their friends are. I just look 'em in the eye and I can tell the bad ones."

Bolan stared at the sunburned skin at the back of the driver's neck. A thin white scar curved up from under the collar, climbed his neck like a vine and disappeared into the thick mat of gray hair. Looked like a knife cut.

"So, like I'm looking at you and thinking, 'He looks tough enough, all right. Real tough.' But tough ain't exactly mean. Not the same thing at all. And most these bums got that *mean* look. Know what I'm sayin', son?"

"Uh-huh," Bolan said. "You think I'm pretty."

The driver sighed, shook his head sadly. "Then

again, if I knew anything I wouldn't be driving this damn car spending all my mornings with criminals, would I?"

"Guess not," Bolan said. He hated to come on so rough with the old cop, but he didn't want anybody getting the idea he was anything other than what he was pretending to be: a hardened career criminal. But, yeah, he knew what the driver meant because Bolan had seen the same look himself in the scum he'd been dealing with these past years. That arrogance in the expression, as if nothing else in the world mattered but what they wanted. As if there was no greater good than satisfying their enormous appetites.

Yeah, he'd seen that look, even managed to blow it off a few choice faces. Now he had to wear it himself. The sneer, the swagger, the cruel talk.

The driver's overweight partner opened the car door and climbed in, a clipboard in one hand, two doughnuts in the other. "Here, Gus," he said, handing one to the driver. "Jelly, just the way you like."

"Thanks, Deke," Gus said, nodding, taking a big bite, licking the jelly from his lips. He gestured over his shoulder at Bolan. "What about him?"

"Hell, it was tough enough wrangling these two. Those guys are more interested in guarding their doughnuts than this gate." He fastened his seat belt. "Besides, Gus, you'd think that damn scar on your neck woulda taught you what happens when you care too much about these cons."

Gus shrugged, accelerated the squad car through the open gate.

Despite himself, Bolan felt a sense of relief as they passed through the gate. As if tight metal bands had been snipped from his chest. He took a deep breath. Better not get too used to that feeling, he warned himself. In case things go wrong.

"They did it again," Deke said, chuckling.

"Did what?" Gus asked.

"Last night, they hit Clip Demoines's bookie joint down in Augusta. Those guys at the gate were telling me about it. Broke in and trashed the place."

"Cops?"

"No, them night riders. The ones the papers are calling Savannah Swingsaw."

"Jeez."

"Yup. They chewed that place up with chain saws and axes, took the money and closed the joint down for good."

"Demoines," Bolan interrupted. "Isn't he the local Mafia kingpin?"

"As if you didn't know," Deke sneered, munching on his doughnut, crumbs powdering his chin.

"Maybe this guy's not local," Gus said, referring to Bolan. "Don't sound local, anyway." Gus caught a yellow light and gunned the car through it. "Yeah, Demoines is connected. Runs most of Georgia, from Atlanta to Savannah. But not for long, not if this Savannah Swingsaw keeps up the pressure."

"Just some other thugs muscling in," Deke said.

"Not likely," Gus said. "Don't act like no Mob I've ever seen. All dressed in black with hoods, like them Oriental ninjas. 'Cept these guys carry guns and axes and chain saws."

"Guns or not," his partner said, "I'd hate to be in their hoods when Demoines's hoods catch up with 'em. I've seen some bodies he's ordered extinct. Hardly qualify as human afterward." He gobbled down the last bite of doughnut.

"Well, the Swingsaw's hit him three times so far. Managed to get away each time without a scratch."

"Just a matter of time, Gus. Time and manpower, and Demoines has got plenty of both."

"That's true. Only this Swingsaw bunch seems to know its way around these Mob types. Kinda like that Mack Bolan fella used to."

At the mention of his name Bolan looked up, startled. He listened to the conversation for a moment, then settled back into his seat, unconcerned.

The Executioner was a master of role camouflage. It had worked for him in Nam many times, dressed as a peasant in a paddy, while the enemy walked by a few feet away, none the wiser. But sometimes no disguise is the best. The brain doesn't register what the eyes see. Now, as Bolan listened to the good-natured bantering in the front seat, he realized this was one of those times.

"Hell, that guy was nuts, man. Taking on cops and the Mob."

"Maybe," Gus said. "And you know I don't condone no vigilante behavior. Only this Bolan, he was different. Seemed to know the difference between the law and justice. Wasn't afraid to do something about it, neither."

"Don't matter. He was then and this is now, Gus."

"Could be this Savannah Swingsaw *is* Mack Bolan. Same MO. And word's gotten around he ain't dead at all, like they was saying before."

Bolan rapped his handcuffs against the screen. "Hey, just where is this Demoines guy located?"

"What's it to you?" Deke asked.

"Might want to look him up when I get out. Guy with that kind of dough might be looking for a few good men. If the price is right."

Deke snorted. "He may not be around when you get out of jail, Blue. If you get out alive, that is."

5

"You know those prison movies where the new fish comes in and his cellmate is this muscle-bound asshole that tells him to take the top bunk or else get his head busted?"

Bolan nodded. "Yeah."

The muscular black man in the wheelchair looked at Bolan menacingly. "Well, you got the top bunk, new fish."

Bolan didn't move. "What if I'm afraid of heights?"

The man rolled his wheelchair to within three inches of Bolan's feet. "How do you feel about a shank in your gut?"

Bolan climbed up to the top bunk, bounced on the thin mattress. "Hmm, not as high as I'd thought."

The black man in the wheelchair grinned. "Well, well, fish. You're a lot smarter than most guys in here. One look at me in this chair and they figure they can take me. All they got to do is maybe tip over my chair or run around behind me. Some tried." He chuckled in a gruff rumble.

Bolan jumped down from the bunk, carrying his toothbrush to the sink. The black man whirled his chair around faster than Bolan thought was possible in the small cell.

He was in his late thirties, but his arms were huge globes of muscles with thick veins crisscrossing his forearms like underground cables. His chest was equally as developed, slabs of dark stone straining at the cotton prison shirt.

Only the legs looked out of place, shriveled stems flopping limply from side to side as he moved the chair.

"My life story isn't any of your business, chump, so don't ask," he snapped, catching Bolan's stare.

"Right," Bolan said. He didn't have to ask. He'd seen men like that before. And there was a look in the man's eyes, the kind of hidden pain recognizable only by someone who'd shared at least a glimmer of that pain.

Bolan splashed some cold water on his eyes and turned to face the man in the wheelchair. "Nam?"

The black frowned with surprise, nodding slowly.

"When?" Bolan asked.

"Sixty-six, near Saigon. We bulldozed some rubber plantations near the Cambodian border."

Bolan nodded. "Operation Cedar Falls."

"Yeah, that's right. You there?"

Bolan hesitated. He heard a hopeful note in the man's voice, but being in Nam wasn't part of the biographical file he and Brognola had created for Damon Blue. If there was going to be any chance at all of this mission succeeding, he'd have to stick to the script. "Nah, I wasn't there. My brother had a friend. He yapped about it all the time."

"Sure," the man in the wheelchair said bitterly. "Everybody had a friend. Shit." He spun his chair around and wheeled forward to the bars. "Just stay outta my face, Blue."

"Fair enough. Only what's your name? I like to know whose face I'm staying out of."

The big man in the wheelchair kept his back to Bolan, his dead knees pressed against the bars. He didn't bother answering.

"LYLE CARREW," Gordon Schultz said. He blew his nose into his napkin, then peeked into the napkin before crumpling it and tossing it onto his lunch tray. "That's his name. Shame about him being crippled and all."

Bolan shrugged, spooned more tomato soup into his mouth. The food wasn't too bad, no worse than most hospitals, but there wasn't enough of it. He'd finished his Salisbury steak and beet salad and had given Gordon Schultz two cigarettes for his soup and half a pack of crackers. The information came free.

Schultz stashed the smokes in his shirt pocket. "Cripple or not," he went on, "the guy can handle himself. Saw him bust the arm of Billy Fieldstone last week. Young Billy's from down Folkston way, that's Okefenokee Swamp land, and he's got a bit of the KKK in his blood. Figured Carrew was an easy target. Learned different real fast."

"What's he in for?"

"Lyle?" Schultz smiled. "He's 'waitin' trial like us. Only he ain't as smart. At least you and me was just practicin' our trade, tryin' to make a buck. You holdin' up the liquor store, me a bank. But Lyle there—'' Schultz chuckled ''—he was just havin' fun. Tore up a whole wing of the V.A. hospital. Dumped files, beat up a doctor, scared the hell outta the nurses. Tossed a desk and a coupla TVs from the eighth-floor window. Took four cops to cuff him. Not bad for a guy in a wheelchair.''

Bolan stopped in midsip and looked across the room to where Lyle was eating at a table by himself. "Has a temper, huh?"

"Damn straight. And that ain't the first time he tore that joint up. Last time he got thirty days. This time, I dunno. If he opens his smartass mouth to the judge...." Schultz shook his head to indicate it would be plenty of time. "They usually keep guys in wheelchairs in the infirmary, but Lyle put up such a fuss, you know, discrimination against the handicapped, that kinda crap, they stuck him in here with the rest of us. Some victory, huh?"

Bolan shrugged. "That's his problem, not mine. He's just my cellmate." He pointed his spoon at a table across the isle where Dodge Reed sat hunched over his ice tea looking frightened. He seemed even younger than in the photograph Hal Brognola had shown him. "What's the kid doing here? Mess up on some fraternity prank?"

"Him? That's, uh, Reed. Got some stupid first name, what is it? Chevy or Ford. Somethin' like that." Schultz laughed. "We got him coupla days ago from the downtown jail. Some kind of embezzlin' from a record store. Kid stuff. Well, he's going to do some growin' up real soon."

Bolan kept his voice bored, indifferent. "Whaddya mean?"

"See that guy over there? The one with the bullet head and the tiny eyes."

Bolan followed Schultz's gaze to a tall lanky man stacking empty trays and glancing possessively at Reed. "Big fella."

"Yeah, about six-six. Strong, too. Name's Bertrand Stovell, but calls hisself Rodeo. He's let it known that the Reed kid is his."

Bolan studied Rodeo from across the room. There was the mean look in the eyes that Gus had talked about.

Tattooed snakes crawled out of each sleeve of his shirt and coiled around his wrists like bracelets. He was completely bald except for one six-inch tail of braided hair at his nape.

Reed glanced up from his tray once and saw Rodeo looking straight at him. Rodeo grinned, showing a set of brown, twisted teeth. Reed frantically looked back into ice tea.

"Rodeo always get what he wants?" Bolan asked.

Schultz snickered. "Mostly. Hell, just look at him. This ain't no federal pen, Blue. Not the Big A or anythin', where they got your hard-core dopers and killers. This is county, mostly made up of nonviolent types who're just pullin' their time, smokin' a little weed now and then. But basically they're just tryin' to get as much good time as possible to get out. They don't want no hassles. Problem is, we got a hell of a lot more cons in Georgia than we got cells, so the Big A, that's the Atlanta pen, been sendin' their overflow here. Screwed everythin' up, man. Those guys got their own rules, their own way of doin' shit, man. The rest of us just stay outta their way. Rodeo wants the Reed kid, fine. Who's gonna stop him? There'll be more tomorrow. One thing this place ain't short on, it's residents.''

IT WAS NEVER DARK.

It was never quiet.

The lights were everywhere, the noise constant.

The hardest part was never being alone. And never being alone meant never feeling safe. It was like being back in the war, but with no place to hide. No jungle underbrush, no heavy darkness.

Bolan's concentration on the problem of protecting Reed and planning their escape was never as complete as he liked because he was always watching his back, checking out any con who came within arm's reach as a potential attacker.

Yet he continued to fine-tune his battle plan, mingling with other cons, gathering information as only those who'd spent time here would know. Together with what he'd learned from Brognola and what he'd been able to observe himself, Bolan had a pretty accurate picture of the place.

Most of the 825 residents were housed in larger cells—two thirty-eight-man dorms, a bunch of sixteen-man cells and a sprinkling of two-to-four-man cells, even a few one-man isolation cells. There were no jobs, but most of the cells had TVs. Still, boredom was the prison's worst enemy, distorting every action, making every grumpy aside a cause for fighting. The atmosphere was tense.

And to make matters worse, the spillover from

other prisons brought an even worse element. The average stay at Fulton had been thirty days, now there were real hard-timers. Contraband had been minimal, now it was rampant. Violence had been under control, now they were imitating Atlanta's policy, where prisoners were killed on ''contracts'' up to $2,000.

Fulton was trying a few reforms to keep the less hardened cons from joining the hard-core punks. More frequent visitation, more recreation. It wasn't working. The really bad guys, like Rodeo, had more power over the average con's life than the entire prison system. That was the first lesson anyone interested in survival learned.

All Bolan had to do was sit in his cell, go to meals and smoke in the exercise yard, keeping a discreet distance from the others but staying close enough to keep an eye on Reed. The rest of the time he perfected his plan. But even with that to occupy his mind, the ceaseless boredom of the place, mixed with the anxiety of watching his back, gnawed at him.

The cell itself was cramped and stark, a little larger than a bathroom. It had bunk beds, two shelves, a sink, a toilet. Most of the other prisoners had decorated their walls with photos of family or ragged-edged pages torn from girlie magazines. Some with paintings or poems they'd done themselves. Lyle Carrew's cell was barren. Nothing adorned the walls. No TV. A hunk of string was stretched between two walls to hold some hand laundry, socks and T-shirt, but that was all. He had a couple of books on the wall shelf, which he told Bolan not to touch unless he wanted to lose an eye.

He wasn't much company either. He sat in his chair or lay on his bunk, either reading one of his books or scribbling in a steno notepad. Bolan tried a couple of ruses to get him to talk, mostly to find out more about the prison routine, the kind of inside info—like which guards sold drugs or were employed by which prisoners—that even Brognola hadn't been able to find out. But Carrew ignored him.

There wasn't much time. Zavlin's deadline for killing Reed was approaching. And to complicate matters, Reed was also in danger from that hardcase Rodeo. Bolan had to get to Reed first.

His first opportunity came in the exercise yard.

Reed was standing against the wall, watching a bunch of cons playing a rough game of three-on-three basketball. One of the guys, with two teardrops tattooed on his cheek, threw the ball at the guy guarding him, but the guy threw the ball back at him and the game went on.

"You play basketball?" Bolan asked Reed, leaning against the wall next to him.

Dodge Reed shifted nervously, looking around the yard for the nearest guard. He mumbled something.

"Huh?" Bolan asked.

"In high school. Played a little, if the team was far enough ahead or the starters all fouled out."

Bolan laughed. "Used to wrestle some myself. That and football."

Reed nodded, relaxing a little, but still tense.

Bolan studied the kid without looking at him. This would be the tough part. Telling him some Russian assassin was after him and would he mind explaining why. That might make Reed bolt and stay away from Bolan, which would make it impossible to protect him. Play it cool for now, Bolan told himself. Take it easy.

"You serving or waiting?" Bolan asked.

"What?" Reed look confused.

"Serving your time or waiting for trial?"

"Waiting for trial. Got held over in the prelim, set to go in two weeks. My lawyer's asked for a postponement." He shrugged. "We'll see."

Bolan saw Lyle Carrew over by the weightlifting area, curling a couple of heavy dumbbells. There were a dozen or more other lifters tugging at the weights, their bodies pumped up with blood and muscle, slick with sweat, glistening in the hot sun like armor. Armor, Bolan thought, just what they're building. Something that warns others to keep their distance. Another wall within the walls.

Bolan saw Carrew look at him, then away again, as if they were strangers.

Bolan also saw Rodeo. Tall, lanky, mean. Walking toward him and Dodge Reed. His sleeves were rolled up and the fat tattooed snakes were more apparent now as they wound their way up his arms, their fanged mouths open and angry on each biceps. Their eyes were red, the only other color against the rest of the blue tattoo.

His bald head reflected the bright sun, the little braid of hair bouncing off the back of his neck.

Rodeo had his thumbs hooked in his pants, cowboy fashion. He wasn't alone. Two other rough-looking guys matched him step for step, though they fell off and waited about ten yards away as Rodeo approached Bolan and Reed.

"Hiya, kid," Rodeo said to Dodge Reed, winking.

Some of the other inmates who'd been standing nearby quickly drifted away. Apparently, Rodeo expected Bolan to do the same, because he suddenly gave him a harsh look.

"You waiting for something, asshole?" Rodeo said to Bolan.

"Yeah," Bolan replied. "A tan. And you're standing in my light."

Rodeo's pale face flushed with rage. His shoulders stiffened. He stepped closer to Bolan, looking down from his six-feet-six-inch height. "You're Damon Blue, right?"

"Yup."

"Done some time in Joliet and Attica?"

"Word gets around."

"To the right people," Rodeo said. "And I'm the right people in this hole. Outside you may have been a tough guy at your local bar or in your bowling league. But in here you're just a piss ant. Got me, Blue?"

"I got a feeling you don't want to be friends."

Reed started sliding slowly along the wall, trying to get away. A big hand with long fingers like squid tentacles clamped around Reed's upper arm. "Not so fast, kid. You and me are gonna get to know each other. Real well. You like grass, man? Scag? Coke? I got it all. Whatever you want.''

Reed shook his head. "N-no, thanks. I don't use anything."

Rodeo laughed. "You will, kid. I'll show you how. Ain't nothing like the first time someone fixes you up. Makes you almost glad to be in here. Stuff's easier to get than outside." He patted Reed on the head. "Yeah, kid, you and me gonna be real good friends."

Reed flinched from the hand on his head, ducking out from under it. That angered Rodeo, who immediately lashed out with an open palm and smacked Reed across the face. The power of the blow bounced Reed's head off the cement wall and left five red welts on his cheek where the fingers had made contact.

"Don't you ever do that again, kid!" Rodeo snarled, his upper lip curled back to reveal those twisted brown teeth. "You piss me off and I'll turn you over to half a dozen guys at once, then slice off an ear and blame it on the blacks. You understand?" He had his big hand around Reed's throat now, squeezing, lifting the kid up onto his toes. There was more strength in that tall lanky frame than it appeared.

Reed's face was turning a little blue as his toes scuttered against the pavement. The angle of the wall made it difficult for the guards to see them, especially with so many cons milling around. The one guard who had perfect sight of them was obviously ignoring them. Bolan had heard from some other cons that Rodeo's drug business at the Big A and here netted him more than $100,000 a year. With that kind of money, he could afford a guard or two.

"I think he's had enough," Bolan said. Reed looked about to pass out.

"Fuck off, man," Rodeo warned.

Bolan fired his right fist into Rodeo's kidney with enough impact to drop the big man to one knee. Rodeo's face contorted with pain as he grabbed his side.

Dodge Reed sagged against the wall, rubbing his throat, sucking in air.

All the prisoners who saw it just stared open-mouthed, then scattered, trying to get away. Except the two badasses who'd accompanied Rodeo. They rushed at Bolan with closed fists and murderous scowls.

The first was about 230 pounds, with short thick arms covered with matted black hair. He tried to wrap them around Bolan's chest, but the Executioner sidestepped him, spun around behind him and rammed his face into the cement wall. The nose popped immediately, spraying a sunburst splotch of blood onto the wall. Bolan kept his hand at the back of the guy's head, grinding it into the rough cement, scraping the skin off his face until he dropped to his knees with a howl.

The second heavy was not as big as the first, but he was faster and smarter. He snapped his knee high into Bolan's lower back, sending a freight train loaded with dynamite rattling up Bolan's spine. The next blow was a rabbit punch, exploding at the base of Bolan's skull with brilliant fireworks. The force of the blow sent Bolan stumbling forward, almost tripping over the first guy, who was still on his knees, dabbing his fingers in blood, feeling for what was left of his face.

Out of the corner of his eye, the Executioner saw Lyle Carrew wheeling his chair toward them. Not in any hurry though. Slowly, as if strolling.

Bolan heard the shuffle of feet as his attacker again lunged at him from behind. Bolan ducked out of the way, tucking in one shoulder and rolling as the hardguy's size-twelve foot came stomping down where Bolan's head had been a moment before, dust puffing around the foot from the impact.

The Executioner stopped his roll and looked up in time to see the man getting ready to jump on his head again. Quickly, Bolan rifled a leg straight out, cracking his heel into the attacker's kneecap. The fragile bone shattered, dropping him to the ground in agony.

Bolan snapped his other heel into the guy's gaping mouth. The hard rubber clipped the row of bottom teeth, popping them out of the gums onto the ground like a handful of white dice.

Rodeo's two henchmen lay moaning, half-conscious.

That left Rodeo, who faced Bolan, one hand pressed to his tender side. His bald head was bumpy in the bright sunlight, the small eyes almost invisible under the dark canopy of his thick eyebrows. He reached inside his waistband and plucked out a nine-inch shank. "You gonna die, asshole. In small pieces."

Behind Rodeo, young Dodge Reed had recovered enough to understand what was going on. He looked at the two writhing men on the ground, the gleaming shiver of sharp metal in Rodeo's hand. Then he attacked.

It wasn't much of an attack, a weak punch to Rodeo's back ribs, as if he was trying to find the same spot where Bolan had hit the prison tough guy. Rodeo barely noticed the punch, whirling fast enough to backhand Reed, knocking him off his feet and spinning back to face Bolan again with his blade.

"That kid's gonna be even sorrier than you, Blue," Rodeo said, grinning. "He's gonna be the whore of some of my guys, who aren't too nice. But then, at least he'll be alive awhile. Not like you."

Rodeo held the shank flat in his hand, the way an experienced knife-fighter would. Bolan spread his arms wide, centering his gravity as he backed up slowly.

From behind him came the creaking of a wheelchair, and Lyle Carrew swung into view, setting the brake on his chair, smiling for the first time since Bolan had met him.

"This I got to see," he said, rubbing his hands together. Rodeo's toothless pal groped around on the ground, trying to pull himself up. Blindly he grabbed Carrew's wheelchair. "Hey, man," Lyle said, hammering him on top of the head with a fist, knocking him back to the ground, dazed. "Hands off," he said.

The first cut came from a fake. Rodeo thrust the blade low toward Bolan's stomach, forcing the Exe-

cutioner to dodge to the left. When he did, Rodeo
whipped the shank upward toward Bolan's exposed
throat. Bolan pivoted in time, but the steel shank
scored, tracing a bloody line across his shoulder.

The slash burned a little, but Bolan ignored it.
He'd fought guys with knives before. Many didn't
know how to use them properly. Those who knew
what they were doing were another matter. Especially when they were that tall.

The hand with the knife teased at Bolan, flicking
out, then pulling back without committing itself.
Bolan watched it, saw the tattooed tail of the snake
coiled around the wrist, the rattles etched onto the
back of the hand.

"Come on, you guys," Carrew encouraged.
"These guards aren't going to play dumb forever."

Rodeo lunged again, the blade torpedoing at
Bolan's heart. Bolan chopped at the wrist, knocking
it away. That blow would have broken an ordinary
man's wrist. Not Rodeo's. He kept coming, thrust-
ing the knife in quick jabs. Bolan leaped out of the
way each time, finally grabbing the wrist and pulling
Rodeo closer, snapping his forehead into Rodeo's
chin, trying to twist the blade out of Rodeo's
hand....

"Guards!" someone whispered.

Rodeo and Bolan pushed apart. There was more
to fear from the guards than from each other. Inmates had all the time in the world to deal with petty
squabbles. But not from solitary confinement.

By the time the guards pushed their way through
the crowd, Bolan and Rodeo were standing far

apart, Bolan helping Reed to his feet, Rodeo nudging his men with his feet.

"What's going on here!" the first guard demanded. "What happened?"

"Basketball," Bolan said. "We were playing. Scrambling for the ball. A wild elbow, you know. Accident."

"No harm, no foul," Rodeo agreed.

"Search 'em," the first guard ordered, throwing all of them up against the wall. They patted each prisoner down, but there were no weapons. Rodeo's blade had been passed on to a friend who was already on the other side of the yard.

The guard pulled Rodeo's heavy henchman to his feet, wincing at the pulpy shredded face. "Holy! Get this one down to the infirmary."

"What about me?" Rodeo's other man asked, his toothless mouth a bloody hole.

"Yeah, you too. Let's go." The first guard hauled them off. But Bolan saw a look pass between the second guard and Rodeo, something like a shrug.

Rodeo nodded and rubbed his hand over his lumpy bald head, fingering his braided tail. He stared down into Bolan's eyes, and growled, "Soon, Blue. Very soon."

6

Bolan leaned over his cell's tiny sink and dabbed some wet toilet paper to the cut on his shoulder. Behind him, Lyle Carrew put on reading glasses and jotted notes in his steno pad.

"Thanks," Bolan said.

Carrew didn't look up. "You talking to me?"

"Yeah. I said thanks."

"For what?"

"For your help out there. Flooring Rodeo's henchman."

Carrew looked up and laughed. "Hell, I wasn't helping you, fish, I was hurting him. Big difference. Bastard touched my chair. I taught him not to."

"Yeah, well, thanks anyway."

Carrew frowned at Bolan. "I don't want you getting the wrong idea, fish. That could be fatal. Nobody around here helps anybody else unless they want something. I don't know what you want from that Reed kid, that's your business. You don't look like you want him the way Rodeo wants him, but either way I don't care. Understand me now."

"Sure. All for none and none for all. That about sums it up?"

"You got a look, man, that says you don't believe

me. Just so we're clear, you and me, and you don't go expecting any help later when Rodeo comes after you, and he will, for sure. Let me show you something.''

Carrew's hands reached back into the mechanism of his chair, fiddled with something and suddenly there was a flat blade in his hand, eight inches long, sharpened on both sides.

"See? Now if I really wanted to help you out there, I'd have tossed you this. Am I right?''

Bolan nodded. "Thanks for straightening me out. I'd hate to go another minute thinking maybe you were doing something nice.''

Lyle Carrew replaced his shank in its hiding place and wheeled toward Bolan. "You're a weird guy, Blue. I know your rap sheet, and I've seen you handle yourself damn well out there. You been inside before, you know how things work.''

"I'm sentimental,'' Bolan sneered.

"You're something. I haven't figured out what. Yet.''

Bolan glanced at his wound. The bleeding had stopped. He shrugged back into his shirt and thought of how he could get to Dodge Reed. Now with Rodeo and his gang after both of them, he'd have to make his break soon. Real soon.

To make matters worse, Carrew's curiosity was aroused. The man in the wheelchair was sharp, perceptive. The slightest hint that a prisoner might not be what he appeared could send a shiver of paranoia through the prison population that would result in a shank buried in his back within the hour. Cops had gone undercover in prisons before. When discovered, they didn't live long.

Carrew was peering over the rims of his glasses at Bolan. The glasses made him look oddly bookish. "You aren't talking now, Blue. You got something to hide?"

Bolan acted angry. "What's your problem, man? Shit, you go around here acting like you've done twenty years of a life term. Telling me how it is. Who not to trust. Hell, all you did was punch out a doctor and scare some nurses. Big goddamn deal."

Carrew chuckled. "Seemed like one to them."

"Yeah, well that kind of prankish crap don't cut it in here. Most of the guys are in here because they've wanted something and they were willing to rob or hurt or kill to get it. What you did didn't get you nothing."

"That's a fact," Carrew said, folding his glasses and tossing them on his bunk. "You probably think I'm just some crazy black with a chip on his shoulder about his color or being crippled or both."

"Are you?"

Carrew shrugged. "Maybe. Yeah, maybe I'm just a bitter vet. Or bitter about being black. You want a fact, Blue? Something that'll knock your socks off? Here's a statistic for you. In the U.S. an inmate has a one in 3,300 chance of being killed during one year in prison. But the average black man outside prison stands a 1 in 1,700 chance. That means he's at twice the risk of being killed *outside* jail. Yeah, that might make me bitter, make me toss a few TVs out of a window."

Those were damn good reasons to be bitter, Bolan thought, but that didn't seem to be Carrew's problem. He was smart enough to go beyond what couldn't be changed, work on what could. The books and weightlifting showed that.

"Everybody's got problems, Carrew," Bolan said.

Carrew looked Bolan in the eyes. A slow grin spread across his face. "You're not buying that as my motive, are you?"

"Nope."

"Good. You didn't strike me as the kind of guy who'd take much whining. All right, Blue, just for the sake of killing some time, I tell you the truth." He leaned back in his wheelchair and sighed. "Ever follow college football back in the sixties, Blue?"

"Some."

"Heisman Trophy winners?"

Bolan nodded.

"Who got it in 1966?"

"I don't remember. What's the point?"

"Dick Kazmaier, Princeton."

"So?" Bolan asked.

Carrew chuckled. "Yeah. So what, huh? That was almost twenty years ago. That was then and this is now. Only there was another football player back then, a year earlier, who'd come so close that everyone agreed he would win that damn Heisman for sure the following year. It would be *his* year." Carrew grinned.

Now Bolan stared in sudden recognition. "Lyle 'In Style' Carrew. Penn State."

Carrew grinned brightly. "That's me. Aren't you going to ask what happened?"

Bolan finished buttoning his shirt, not saying anything.

Carrew continued. "Anyway, our boy Lyle ended up in Nam in '66, making end runs with grenades, getting his legs shot to hell. Spends three months in a POW camp with no doctor, no medical treatment. Only reason they didn't kill him was they liked to watch him crawl across the room for his food. And I crawled, man, crawled for every bite. I learned something about prisons there, man. Anyway, so much for Lyle 'In Style' Carrew's career in the N.F.L."

He laughed that gruff, humorless scraping sound.

"So every once in a while during the N.F.L. draft season I'm a little cranky. I'm in that damn VA hospital, waiting for over an hour, listening to some doctor who was still shitting in diapers in '66, calling me 'Lyle' like I was his son, but getting huffy when I call him 'Dave,' telling me he prefers to be called 'Dr. Donnelly.' So I tossed him into the X-ray machine. Things got a little carried away from there."

Bolan laughed.

"Yeah."

"So what do you do when you're not busting up VA hospitals?"

"Teach kids about the tribal rites of the Aruntas when they'd much rather be groping each other in their dorm rooms. I'm a professor of anthropology at the university."

"You're kidding?"

"Not at all."

"How come they don't fire you for this?"

Carrew laughed. "Tenure. Besides, they need me for other reasons. Aside from being a brilliant instructor and a minor authority in my field, I'm good advertising. They like showing me off as their equal-opportunity employee. Here's our crippled, black, war-veteran professor. Hell, I'm an institution."

Carrew fell silent for a moment. Suddenly he wheeled around, facing the bars, his back to Bolan. "Rodeo's going to kill you, Blue. Going to do it soon, just as he promised. Probably won't come at you alone."

"For a college professor, you sure know a lot about prison survival."

"Three months as a POW, then eight months in a VA hospital, Blue. In some ways the hospital was worse. Not because of the staff, most of whom were terrific. But over there I saw guys struggle against impossible odds and survive, only to come home to a VA hospital and kill themselves within six weeks. Loss of hope is powerful stuff, man. Now I'm a black man in a wheelchair. That's two life sentences. I know how to play rough to survive."

Bolan believed him.

"I also know enough not to get involved in your beef. I gave the cops a hard time when they arrested me, which is why I'm in here. But when things cool down and I roll in front of the judge in my suit and tie and diplomas and medals, promising never to do such a thing again, I'll be back on campus watching the girls get younger every year. In other words, you're on your own."

Bolan grinned. "Always have been, Lyle."

"Yeah." Carrew nodded. "I had a feeling."

They heard the guards' boots clomping along the metal catwalks outside their cell. Bolan and Carrew were on the first tier, to accommodate Carrew's wheelchair. The guards on each tier were selecting the first shift for open visitation, visitors and prisoners mingling in the courtyard.

"This happens on Sundays only," Carrew explained, "and then only for the least threatening residents. Something new."

The guard strolled by their cell and pounded his hickory baton on the bars. "Let's go. You got visitors."

Carrew wheeled to the bars and waited. The doors on the whole row would be opened simultaneously.

"Enjoy," Bolan said, hopping up on his bunk.

"You bet," Carrew said.

"You, too, Blue. Got a visitor. Move it."

"Me?"

"That's what I said. And change that shirt. It's torn."

Bolan was surprised as he jumped down from the bunk, changed shirts and waited at the cell door next to Carrew. A visitor would mean Brognola. And he would only come if there was bad news. Bolan couldn't imagine things being much worse than they already were.

He was wrong.

7

"Trouble," Brognola said, frowning. "*Big* trouble."

Bolan laughed. "Is there any other kind?"

"Not for us, I guess. Sort of comes with the territory." The big Fed popped an antacid tablet into his mouth and chewed. He had a pained expression at first, but after a few minutes, he began to look better.

Bolan led him silently to a far corner of the compound courtyard, on a patch of brown grass desperate for water. Bolan gestured at the pack of tablets. "When did you start with those?"

"These?" Brognola shrugged, looked a little embarrassed and slipped them into his jacket pocket. "Something I ate."

Bolan gave him a patient look.

"Okay, okay. I've been having a little stomach problem for a couple months now."

"About the same time Stony Man Farm was destroyed. And April killed."

Bolan looked sympathetically at his friend. Yeah, things had been tough on the Executioner, but he could see where they might even be tougher on Hal, who was left to deal with the stress of working within the system, yet still helping Bolan underground.

At least when Bolan got mad, he could get even directly. Grab the AutoMag and blast the bad guys to hell. But Brognola couldn't. He had to keep it all bottled up.

"I didn't come here to talk about my stomach," Brognola said gruffly. "We have a small matter of assassination to discuss."

"Go ahead."

"He's here. Zavlin."

Bolan's jaw clenched. "Here where? In the prison?"

"Maybe. He was spotted in Atlanta five hours ago."

Bolan looked around the courtyard at the other prisoners, scrutinizing each face.

"That won't help," Brognola said. "He could be any of them, male or female."

"Yeah, you're right. I know about all that master-of-disguise crap. Expert with makeup and forged documents." Bolan kept scanning the compound. "There are a few things that usually aren't disguised because most people don't pay close enough attention, but...." Bolan saw Lyle Carrew over by a wooden picnic table, talking to a woman. They were both staring at Bolan.

The Executioner felt a strange chill at the nape of his neck. The woman was looking at him with a hard intensity, studying him, not flinching from his gaze. At the same time there was something familiar about her. He didn't recognize her exactly; she had the kind of looks you didn't easily forget. Her hair was long and raven black, dipping to a sharp widow's peak on her forehead.

She was wearing oversize sunglasses despite a cloudy sky. Her mouth was straight, the lips full. The combination produced a pouty smirk that was exceptionally attractive.

Her body was even more exceptional, not just slim and shapely. What was revealed by her short sleeves and shorts proved to be tanned and toned, with sinewy muscles outlined like a relief map of rough terrain. They looked like long smooth sand dunes along a wet beach.

She was perhaps the most striking woman Bolan had ever seen.

And she was still staring at him, saying something to Carrew, who was digging into her picnic basket, biting into some corn bread, shrugging or replying to her.

"You know her?" Brognola said, a hint of admiration creeping into his voice.

"I know the guy with her. My cell mate."

"Looks like he knows how to handle himself."

Bolan nodded. "In more ways than one."

"Where's Reed?"

"Behind us about fifty yards. Talking with his girlfriend."

"How's he holding up?"

Bolan told him about Rodeo. The fight. The threats.

"Hell!" Brognola popped another antacid tablet. "In here one day and you've already got the

meanest mother in the place after you. I know you
work fast, but—''

"Couldn't be helped. Put a fresh-faced kid like
Dodge Reed in here and something was bound to
happen. Besides, it was a good way to get him to
trust me.''

"Fine. Only how are you going to bust out of
here? I could still pull a few strings, get some of-
ficial cooperation—''

Bolan held up his hand. "Won't work, guy. Zavlin could sniff that out in a second. It's got to be
real. Don't worry about me. I've got a couple ideas.
We should be out by tomorrow.''

"What about Rodeo and his bunch?''

"I'll try to keep away from them.''

Brognola looked skeptical. "Try hard. As much
as I'd like to see that scum scraped away, that kid is
our first priority.''

They both looked over at Dodge Reed, whose
hands waved animatedly, his face aged with fear, as
he obviously was describing his harrowing adventures. He even pointed at Bolan, and the pretty
petite girl turned and looked at him, meeting his
eyes and smiling a shy thanks.

Bolan smiled back.

Brognola and Bolan discussed a few more details
until the buzzer blared the end of visitation. Prisoners and visitors alike were herded through metal
detectors, then prisoners were led aside to be body-
searched for drugs or weapons.

Some couples clung to each other, wringing the
most from their last kiss for another week. Reed

and his girlfriend were one of those couples. Bolan could see the tears tracking along her cheeks and felt sorry for both of them. To his credit, Reed gave her an encouraging smile and assured her he'd be fine.

Lyle Carrew and his female companion had already gone through the doors, but Bolan could still see her lingering with the crowd, watching him, making up her mind about something. By the time he and Brognola went through the door she was gone.

"Take care," the Fed said sincerely. "And remember. He could be inside already."

"Yeah," Bolan said. "I'll be looking for him."

8

"You ask too many questions, man."

Bolan shrugged. "I've got a curious nature."

"In here that could be a fatal condition," Carrew warned.

"I simply asked who the woman was you were talking to."

"Simple, hell. I'm trying to avoid any fallout that might come from being your cell mate. If you turn out to be a snitch, they might think I knew something about it."

Bolan didn't bother denying anything. Carrew was too sharp to bullshit. Let him think what he wanted. Within the next two hours, with a little luck, he and Reed would be out of here. He'd worked out most of the details in his mind. The one problem: getting Reed to go along. Bolan hadn't yet explained anything to the kid. What good would it do? Even if Reed believed him, would he risk busting out of jail? Probably not. So Bolan was going to have to take him along anyway.

By force.

"Why all this interest in her, anyway?" Carrew asked.

"She looked vaguely familiar, that's all."

"Yeah? You think because we had a little fireside chat about my past we're buddies now? Forget it, man."

Bolan shook his head. "I just asked her name, Carrew."

"Funny thing," the black man said, frowning. "Because she asked yours, too."

Bolan waited for more, but Carrew didn't offer anything. "What'd she say when you told her?"

"Said she could be wrong, but you reminded her of someone else, someone she knew a long time ago."

Bolan tried to think, picturing her gorgeous face, the trim body. A name hovered in the distance, out of sight. He had to stop thinking about it, concentrate on the escape. There were too many things that might go wrong for him to allow any distractions. He retied his shoelaces in double knots. There would be some running tonight.

"Said she didn't recognize the name, though. Damon Blue."

"I've used lots of names," Bolan said. "She think what name she knew?"

Carrew returned his concentration on the book he was reading when Bolan interrupted him.

Outside the cell, men milled back and forth. The cell doors were open for all the minimum security prisoners, giving them a chance to mingle before lights-out for the night.

Bolan headed for the open cell door. "See you later, Lyle."

Carrew looked up. "I wouldn't go out there, man. You're marked."

"Rodeo's not minimum security. He's supposed to be locked up."

"Big difference between 'supposed to be' and 'is.'"

Bolan knew that, but he had to check on Dodge Reed, make sure the kid was okay for the next couple of hours. "Thanks for the warning."

Carrew shrugged. "Just looking out for myself."

"Yeah, right." Bolan was about to leave when a shark-faced guard blocked the doorway, chewing gum noisily.

He slapped his baton into his palm and nodded at Bolan. "Come with me, Blue."

"Where?" Bolan said. He recognized the guard as the one who'd exchanged glances with Rodeo out in the courtyard, the one who'd ignored the fight.

"You don't ask no questions around here, Blue," the guard barked. "You do what you're told. Now haul ass, mister."

Bolan started for the door, tripped over Carrew's wheelchair and fell sprawling to the floor next to the chair.

"Shit, man," Carrew complained, almost getting knocked over.

"Sorry," Bolan said, climbing to his feet, his hand pressed against his chest as if he'd bruised something.

"Don't get nervous now, Blue," the guard taunted with a chuckle, chewing his gum rapidly. "We ain't going to no gas chamber."

"Aren't you?" Carrew said.

"Watch yourself, Carrew. You don't want none of his trouble, do ya?"

Carrew stared angrily at the guard, then looked up at Bolan. "Like I said before, man. You'll have to help yourself."

"I just did," Bolan said. His back was to the guard as he opened his fist clutched to his chest. In it was Carrew's shank, which Bolan had taken from the wheelchair when he'd fallen. He stuffed it down his shirt.

"You mother," Carrew said, groping under the seat of his chair, finding nothing. He looked angry enough to lunge at Bolan, but the Executioner was already falling in step next to the gum-chewing guard.

The other prisoners looked away as the two men marched by, as if they didn't want to be able to testify later.

Once they were out of sight of the open cells, the guard threw Bolan up against the wall, pressing his baton into the base of Bolan's skull as he frisked him. He pulled Carrew's shank out of Bolan's shirt. "Been a bad boy, Blue."

"Just something to sew my torn shirt."

He shoved Bolan ahead of him as they continued down the hallway.

Bolan watched the guard unlock the door to the corridor for solitary confinement cells. They were hardly ever used to lock up prisoners, though they were a popular spot for boozing, shooting up or just passing a joint around.

"What's this all about?" Bolan asked innocently.

"Whaddya think, fish?"

"Maybe my pardon came from the governor?"

"Yeah," the guard snorted, "I want ya to meet the governor and his staff."

He prodded Bolan ahead of him down the dim hallway. The doors on either side began opening. Three rough-looking men with shanks stood sneering at Bolan. And finally at the end of the walkway, Rodeo stepped out, his fists fitted with heavy brass knuckles with sharp one-inch spikes protruding from each knuckle.

9

"Wait outside," Rodeo told the guard, who grinned and left. The door closed behind him with a hollow thud.

Bolan was silent. He eyeballed each man carefully, analyzing from the way they moved what their strengths and weaknesses were. He didn't find many weaknesses.

The three men faced Bolan in the narrow corridor like a wall of malignant flesh, their hard thick bodies tense and bristling. The flat, crudely made blades shone dully in their hands.

Behind them, Rodeo chuckled.

There was no way out. On the other side of the door, their bribed guard was waiting. On this side, three armed bone-crushers and one bald giant with spikes on his knuckles.

Some choice.

"You boys can cut him up some," Rodeo was telling them, "but I want him alive." He hoisted his studded knuckles. "For these. My tenderizers."

Bolan fell into his combat stance, feet apart, weight evenly distributed. The corridor was too narrow for any fancy moves, but if he could get the knife away from one of those guys, he might just have a chance. Slim, but a chance.

The first to step forward was the heavy one with the matted hair on his arms and neck, the one whose face Bolan had ground to guacamole dip earlier that day. The nose was pushed to the left now with blood crusted darkly at each nostril. Raw tracks swirled across his face where the skin had been raked away.

"Easy, Bradley," Rodeo cautioned. "Watch him."

Bradley lumbered forward, his long blade stabbing the air in front of Bolan. Bolan backed up, keeping a few feet between him and Bradley. He watched the hands, the shank flipping back and forth between them as the man with the raw face tried to catch Bolan by surprise.

"Get his nuts," one of the other guys encouraged. The third man nodded, but didn't say anything. He was the one whose teeth Bolan had kicked out.

Bolan glanced over his shoulder at the thick glass window in the door. The guard who'd escorted him here had his face pressed against the glass. He was grinning, chewing his gum excitedly. He reminded Bolan of those guys who like to watch dogfights, cheering the dogs on until one has gnawed through the other's throat, leaving his dying body convulsing in the dirt.

"Come on, big man," Bradley said. His eyes looked huge and white set in that pulpy skinless face. His knife tattooed the air in front of Bolan's face.

The Executioner backed up another step, but there

was only three feet between his back and the door. He didn't want to get cornered here, so he had to make his move. Soon.

He feinted to the left, then kicked up his right foot, trying to catch Bradley's knife hand. But this time the heavy man was ready. He pivoted away from Bolan's foot and slashed at it with his shank. The knife caught Bolan low on the shin, slicing through his heavy pants and socks, plowing open a furrow of skin all the way to the bone. Bolan felt the blade's bite, the blood soaking into his sock.

Bradley's eyes lit up when he realized he drew blood.

Bolan could swear the man began to drool as he grew even hungrier for more. He plunged forward, a little too anxiously, his shank flicking upward toward Bolan's face. The Executioner yanked himself back just as the blade hissed by his right eye. Then he ducked under the knife, knocked Bradley's arm into the wall and drove his fist straight into the fat man's throat.

Bradley managed to tuck his chin down enough to deflect much of the punch's power, but still he staggered back from the blow, flopping against the door of one of the solitary confinement cells.

He clutched at his throat with one hand, rasping while his other hand swung his knife at Bolan like a scythe. He moved toward Bolan on unsteady legs, his knife arcing back and forth, sizzling through the humid air.

Bolan was backing up again. The shank nipped closer and closer to his stomach. Behind him, the door was only two feet away, the guard grinning through the glass.

Bolan looked up from the probing knife into Bradley's savaged face. The scab tracks made him look even wilder, almost deranged.

C'mon, Bolan thought, this isn't where it all ends. Not yet. Not here. Too much to do. For Hal, for April. For himself. The Executioner shrugged off the defeatist thoughts. He parried a quick thrust from Bradley and decided he'd played the guy's game long enough.

With no weapon and no place to run, he took a giant step back, his shoulders bumping into the door, then slid under the chopping blade, knocking Bradley's thick legs out from under him. The knifer toppled over and Bolan was on him like flames on gasoline. He twisted the shank out of the dazed man's hand, lifted the blade over his head with both hands and plunged it into Bradley's chest, puncturing the heart. Blood sprayed up over his hands and along his forearms. The struggling body went flaccid beneath him and he yanked the bloody knife out and faced Rodeo and his two men.

They stood unmoving.

Bolan glanced over his shoulder and saw the guard was no longer peering in the window. Had he gone to get help? No time to worry about that now. Bolan still had three armed men to face, and they weren't going to make the mistake of coming at him one at a time.

The door behind him burst open and Lyle Carrew sat there in his wheelchair, shaking his head at what he saw. "A party and no one invited me?" He rolled through the door, his wheels running over the hands of the unconscious guard.

"Stay out of this, Carrew," Rodeo said. "Ain't none of your business."

"I don't know about that, man. This fella stole my shank, then lets your bozo guard take it away from him. Guy like that needs a lesson."

Rodeo smiled, fingered his braided hair. "Just what he's about to get. You welcome to join in, get a piece."

Carrew tapped his shank against his palm, thinking. "Nah, I guess not. Guess I'll just take him back to the cell and handle it my way."

"No way," the toothless henchman growled.

"Boone's right, Carrew. You best get your ass the hell out of here. Otherwise you're buying his trouble. That what you want?"

"Nope. It surely isn't." He backed up into the doorway, his wheelchair holding the door open, but blocking any exit. He dropped his shank into his lap, then began tugging at the armrest of his chair. It popped free. "I told this big dumb guy that he was on his own. That you'd be eating his liver for dinner."

"What're you doing?" Rodeo asked, stepping closer.

"I warned him. Didn't I warn you, Blue?"

"You warned me," Bolan said.

Carrew nodded. "See? I warned him." He pulled a piece of the aluminum tubing free from the chair. It was about a foot long. Then he began dismantling some of the spokes from the large wheel of his chair. They popped right out. "Me, I'm only in for a few days, maybe a few weeks, depending on how pissed that judge is that I yelled at. Contempt of court, no big deal. Am I right?"

"He's right," Bolan said to Rodeo.

Carrew twisted the spokes into six-inch lengths. They looked to Bolan as if they'd been specially made that way, to break into those sections. Carrew leaned over the side of his chair and pried the unconscious guard's mouth open, probing inside with his fingers, then smiled when he found what he was looking for. The wad of chewing gum.

"What the hell you doing?" Rodeo snarled.

"Minding my own business, man. The only difference is...." He tore a hunk of gum from the wad, rolled it into a ball between his thumb and fingers, then stuck it on the end of one of the wire spokes. He inserted the spoke into the cylinder, put the tube to his mouth and pointed it at toothless Boone.

Carrew sucked in his breath, and puffed his cheeks out as he blew into the tubing. The makeshift dart whooshed down the corridor and pierced Boone's throat just below the Adam's apple.

Boone's eyes widened with surprise as his hands flew to the spike and plucked it out. He started to speak, but the words came out in a croak. Blood was seeping from the little hole in his neck, leaking air, puffing pink foam around the hole.

"As I said," Carrew continued, "the only difference is that I'm shaving the odds a bit. Little trick I learned from an Indian tribe in South America.''

Boone dropped his shank, clutching his hand around the hole in his throat, gasping for air. He started for the door, his interest in this fight over.

''Where you going, Boone?'' Rodeo demanded.

''Doc. . . tor,'' Boone croaked.

''No one leaves!''

But Boone stumbled ahead. Suddenly Rodeo leaped at him, grabbed the back of Boone's shirt and smacked him in the back of the head. The tiny brass studs punched through the skin and hair, drilling through the bone. The momentum of the blow caved in the whole base of the weakened skull. Boone's knees buckled and he fell face first onto the floor. Blood bubbled out the back of his head and sieved through his oily hair.

''You wanted fair,'' Rodeo rasped, ''you got fair. Two against two. Me and Sanders against you and Blue.''

''Not exactly what I had in mind,'' Carrew said, loading another spoke into his tube and puffing it into the face of Rodeo's lone remaining henchman, Sanders.

The dart drilled through the cheek, enough to scare him but not enough to do him serious damage. But while Sanders was plucking it out, Bolan let fly his shank down the eight-foot-long corridor. It flipped end over end like a propeller until it finally thudded solidly into Sanders's chest. Sanders looked down at the protruding shank for a second, more annoyed than anything else, then suddenly his legs melted out from under him and he was sitting on the floor, leaning against the wall. He tried to speak, but his tongue flopped inside his mouth like a beached dolphin. He died trying to pull the knife out of his chest.

"Now this is what I call fair," Carrew said. "One on one. And I'm out of it. Go ahead."

Rodeo looked suspicious. "You ain't gonna help him?"

"No." Carrew looked into Bolan's eyes. "I've got a feeling he wouldn't have it any other way."

Bolan smiled. "You read people pretty well."

"Okay, okay. Then let's get on with it," Rodeo said. "You giving him your shank?"

Carrew shook his head. "No." Then he turned to Bolan. "I told you you were on your own."

The two gladiators squared off in the concrete arena, circling each other. The Executioner's heart was pounding and his fists were clenched. Not out of fear, but determination. The crazy thing was that, yeah, he really did want to fight it out now. Even his short stay in the prison had gotten to him. Despite his planning and information gathering for the escape, the inactivity of the place, the damned boredom, combined with the constant tension, had taken something out of him. Sapped his energy, his fierce drive. Now he was getting it back.

Somewhere out there, maybe even inside the prison, getting closer every minute, was Zavlin, the master assassin out to exterminate some poor kid who was sitting shivering in his cell. Inside that kid's head was something that was a threat to the

KGB and Bolan had to know what that was. And soon.

The only thing in his way was this bald, six-foot-six maniac with the studded knuckle-dusters.

Bolan wanted him.

Bad.

Lying on the floor between Bolan and Rodeo were the three bodies of Rodeo's dear friends. Two of their shanks were on the floor, the third buried deep in Sanders's chest.

Bolan was about to make a dive for Boone's shank, when Rodeo attacked, hurdling his fallen buddies as if they were piles of dirt. He screamed through clenched teeth, stampeding at Bolan like a madman, his braided tail trailing like a flag.

Bolan kept his eyes on Rodeo's hands, the brass studs winking in the light. He'd managed to drop the giant once before, but that was when he'd taken him by surprise. This time there would be no such advantage.

Rodeo was right in front of him now, swinging a roundhouse that could demolish a tree. Bolan ducked under it and the fist swished overhead, smashing into the wall. The studs chipped four holes into the concrete.

Bolan angled past him toward the only shank not near Rodeo. The one nailed into Sanders's chest. The Executioner somersaulted down the corridor, rolling to his feet beside the body. Sanders's hands were still gripped around the shank where he'd tried to dislodge it. Bolan pulled at the hands, trying to loosen the fingers.

No time.

Rodeo was on him again, swinging those lethal fists. Bolan sprang to his feet, bobbing and weaving a couple of punches. He stepped inside one left hook and pounded Rodeo in the cheek. The giant's cheekbone shifted slightly, the skin ripping along the bone. A lightning bolt of blood etched down his cheek.

Rodeo was more cautious now, holding his fists up, but not wasting any energy on wild flurries. He seemed determined to make each punch count. The tattooed snakes seemed fatter and meaner as the muscles in his arms flexed.

Bolan backed up, away from Sanders and the shank. Now the blades were all at the other end of the hall, along with the exit. He'd have to go through Rodeo to get to them.

Bolan didn't expect any more help from Lyle, didn't really want any.

Carrew had seen that this was Bolan's fight, that Bolan was fighting more than just one man, more than just Rodeo. He was fighting what Rodeo was, what he stood for. Despite all appearances about "Blue"—the phony identity, the criminal record—Carrew had been able to see that much. Even now Bolan knew Lyle was probably debating with himself, tempted to toss him a shank, or spit a dart into Rodeo's neck. But Bolan didn't want his help now.

It had nothing to do with any adolescent notions of bravery, of proving himself or showing his cause was the stronger. He knew being right wasn't always enough, didn't always win battles. Yet sometimes there were doors you had to enter alone, maybe for no other reason than you didn't want to.

This was one door he was going through. Without knocking.

"Come on, Blue," Rodeo taunted, closing in. "Let me see what you got."

Bolan stopped backing away, squared his shoulders.

Rodeo grinned. "I'm going back out there with your eyeballs stuck on the ends of these knuckles. Two from you, two from your black friend."

Bolan shrugged. "With that many eyes, maybe you'll be able to see this coming next time." And he snapped a front kick straight into Rodeo's chest. The chest bones dented inward as three ribs cracked from the impact.

Rodeo doubled over, and Bolan threw a right hook and left uppercut combination that rocked Rodeo back into the wall. Blood seeped out over his lip and down his chin. It looked as if he'd been chewing raw meat.

The Executioner tried a spinning kick into the kneecap to disable him, but Rodeo was ready this time. He flung himself off the wall and swung his right fist at Bolan's temple. The Executioner managed to raise his left arm to block the punch, but the brass spikes punctured his arm at the triceps. Pain flamed through the arm, numbing it from wrist to shoulder. When he pulled away, he saw Rodeo grinning, holding his triumphant fist high. Blood capped each brass spike like melting red snow.

"Come here, little eyeballs," Rodeo sneered, stalking closer.

Bolan's left arm was useless. He still had no weapon. And the damage he'd done to Rodeo so far was minor, barely slowing him down.

He looked past Rodeo and saw Carrew loading another dart into his blowpipe. He was tempted to say nothing, pretend he didn't even see it. Right now a dart in Rodeo would be just the distraction he'd need.

Carrew placed the pipe to his lips, stared into Bolan's eyes.

And Mack Bolan shook his head. No.

Carrew hesitated, then lowered the pipe.

Bolan had no intention of losing this fight. He'd fought tougher, smarter opponents before. He'd been a prisoner before. But being in prison, the institution, had dulled him. The boredom had allowed the possibility of failure to creep into his thoughts. What if he failed? He'd be locked in here for years. He'd never worried about the consequences of a mission before. But this time he had without even being aware of it.

No more.

He forced a cold wind through his mind, a cleansing bracing breeze.

Rodeo stepped in for another attack. His looping right glanced off Bolan's shoulder, the brass teeth biting a chunk of flesh from the shoulder. Bolan ignored the pain, stepping closer to Rodeo, slipping under a punch, wrapping his right arm around Rodeo's waist, pulling the giant up over his hip and flinging him to the ground.

Without pause, Bolan loaded all his weight into one knee and dropped full force onto Rodeo's breastbone, cracking it like a lobster's shell. Rodeo's eyes widened with pain and Bolan raised his right hand like a claw above the giant's face. Rodeo's face cringed with terror as the realization of what was about to happen jangled through his brain.

He opened his mouth to scream, but by then Bolan was already moving again, driving his stiffened thumb straight down into Rodeo's right eye, squeezing past the gel of the eyeball, plunging deep into the brain, destroying nervous-system functions. Killing the brain.

Beneath him, Rodeo convulsed slightly, tensed, gagged, relaxed into death with a sigh.

Bolan withdrew the thumb, wiped it on Rodeo's shirt and walked with a slow exhausted gait toward Carrew, stepping over bodies as he walked.

"How do we explain all this?" he asked.

Carrew shrugged. "Mass suicide?"

Bolan smiled grimly as Carrew led him away. The numbness in his left arm was worse. He tried to rub some feeling back into it.

He wasn't too worried about a prison investigation. By the time officials got around to him, he and Reed would already have made their escape. Or would have been shot trying.

"We'd better get back to our cell," Bolan said. Ninety minutes to go before the breakout.

"Sure thing," Carrew said, muscling his wheelchair along. "But there's just one detour we need to make.'' He stopped, spun the chair around to face Bolan.

"Detour?" Bolan asked. "Where?"

Carrew smiled. "That's a surprise."

Bolan felt a little alarm jangle in his head. Something was wrong. He closed his fists and started for Carrew. But he was too late.

The first gunman appeared behind him, the second popped out of the storage closet in front. Both were dressed in black hoods. Each had a Star Model PD .45 pointed at him.

He felt the pinch of a needle as the gunman behind him stabbed his arm with a hypo. There was nothing to do now. Fighting would be useless. They didn't intend to kill him, at least not yet, or they would have done so already. Perhaps they just wanted information. But who were they? How did they get in here? What was Lyle Carrew's connection? What did they. . . ?

Bolan's eyes closed and he dropped endlessly through black space, past the floating bodies of all the friends and enemies who had died violently during the past years. They stared as he dropped past them. Some cried out to him in warning. Others laughed and waved for him to join their ranks.

10

Bolan was conscious but he didn't dare open his eyes. He used his other senses to assess the danger, study his predicament.

He was naked to the waist and could feel the fresh bandages taped to his body. Knife cut on left shoulder, puncture wounds from Rodeo's spiked knuckles on his left triceps, a chunk the size of a rat bite on his right shoulder, the slash across his shin.

A radio played in another room. A commercial for a popular wine. Faintly, Bolan heard a young woman's voice harmonizing with the jingle. She was pretty good.

Onions. He sniffed the tangy scent of cooked onions, his mouth watering involuntarily, his stomach churning from hunger. How long had he been out?

Beneath him, movement. He dug his fingertips into the bed he was lying on and felt the mattress shift like Jell-O. A water bed.

"How long you gonna keep playing this game, Mack Bolan?" a woman's voice drawled. He pedigreed that sassy voice from a lifetime ago.

Bolan opened his eyes and stared into the face of the same beautiful woman he'd seen earlier at the jail with Lyle Carrew.

"Hi, Shawnee," he said.

"Hi yourself." She walked over to the bedroom door, leaned her head out into the hallway and shouted, "He's awake."

Footsteps pattered down the hallway. Three other equally gorgeous women huddled anxiously around the doorway. A leggy blonde, a tall dark-haired woman, a petite Asian. They stared at him as if he was a visitor from another galaxy.

"You all right, Mr. Bolan?" the one with the short blond hair asked. "I hope we didn't hurt y'all none."

Bolan lifted himself up to his elbows. His head was still a little cottony, which the rolling of the water bed didn't help. He nodded at her. "I'm fine."

"Of course he's fine," Shawnee said. "He was in expert hands."

"You stuck me with the needle, right?"

She smiled. "Of course, Mack. You deserve the very best." She turned to the other women. "Okay, you've seen him. Introductions later. Right now Mack and me got some catching up to do." The three women nodded and left. The blonde began singing along with the radio again.

Bolan struggled to the edge of the shifting bed, waiting for the grogginess to clear. It didn't.

"I know what you need," Shawnee said. She sat next to Bolan and began rubbing his neck and shoulders. Her long fingers were hard as the prongs of a rake as they expertly worked his tired muscles, avoiding the bandaged areas. "How's that?"

"Haven't lost the touch, huh?"

"About the only thing I haven't lost."

Bolan looked her up and down appreciatively. Her denim cutoffs and T-shirt didn't hide much. "I noticed. Must be about forty pounds."

"Yep. I'd gained about thirty of them my first year in Nam. That's when we met. Took me years to get rid of them."

"You look good."

"Good? Hell, I look great."

Bolan laughed. "I stand corrected."

"You didn't even recognize me, did you? Admit it. When you saw me at the jail today with Lyle, you didn't know who I was."

"You looked familiar. But it wasn't until I heard your voice just now that I placed a name with the face."

She gave him a serious look, her long black hair intensifying her expression. "It took me a while to place you, too. Had some alterations done to your face, huh?"

"A few. You know why."

"Yeah, I know. Who doesn't? Your name and escapades aren't exactly a national secret. But I heard you'd died."

"Came close enough."

She laughed. "I don't think I ever believed it, though. Not really. Any man who could survive what you did back in Nam—well, he wasn't about to get killed by mere cops or mobsters."

"Nam was a long time ago, Shawnee. We were both a lot younger."

"Dumber. Otherwise you and I wouldn't have

lost touch.'' She paused. ''I guess you know Billy died.''

''I heard.'' Billy was Shawnee's brother, a medic who had served briefly with Bolan before getting wounded by a sniper. Bolan had killed the sniper and carried Billy back to camp and a ''dust-off'' chopper. Billy had been transferred to a Saigon hospital and Bolan had looked him up on a three-day pass.

It was there the Executioner had met Billy's sister, Shawnee, an Army nurse with the 24th Evac Hospital in Tan Sa Nhut. Plump, sassy, intelligent, she and Bolan had become pals, spending most of his three-day pass together, visiting Billy, dining out, just talking. They'd corresponded whenever possible, maintaining their friendship, right up until the day Bolan had come home to bury his father, mother and teenage sister.

The day he stepped out of one war into another.

Shawnee stopped massaging his shoulders.

Bolan stood up. His body felt better now, his strength returning. ''Why'd you bust me out?''

''Why?'' She looked surprised. ''Because, despite your little facial surgery, I recognized you. Your walk, your eyes, your, well, *presence*. Women sense these things. When I asked Lyle about you he told me your name was Damon Blue, so I figured the authorities didn't know who they had yet. But when they did, they'd throw you in the Atlanta penitentiary so fast you'd have bar burns on your palms. And once you were in there, you'd never come out alive. Lots of Mafia guys in the Big A would just love to get their hands on you.''

"Since when do you know anything about breaking people out of jails? That the latest in nurses' training?"

"I'm not a nurse any longer, Mack. Oh, I do some volunteer work at the VA hospital—that's where I met Lyle a couple years ago—but that's all."

Bolan walked over to the window of the bedroom. He pawed aside the curtain and looked out over Atlanta, submerged in darkness. Electric lights glittered as in every big city, though Atlanta had a small-town feeling to it. A fuzzy aura of light seeped up over the horizon. It would soon be dawn.

He faced Shawnee. "You made a mistake breaking me out of jail."

"But—"

"I appreciate the motive, Shawnee, but I was in there for a reason, trying to keep someone alive. Now he's alone and exposed."

"Gee, Mack, I'm sorry. I didn't know."

He placed his rough hand on her cheek. "I know."

"Well, you can't just turn yourself in and claim you were kidnapped. They'd toss you in solitary."

"I wouldn't be much use there."

"So what are you going to do now?"

Bolan frowned. "Only thing I can do, I guess. Break him out, too."

"You'll need help."

"No." Bolan shook his head.

"We got you out, didn't we?" She went to the door and shouted, "Everybody. Come here."

The other three women entered the room.

"About time for introductions, Mack," Shawnee said. "This here is Belinda Hoyt."

Belinda stepped forward with a big smile. Her short blond hair framed her narrow face in a slight tomboy cut. But there was nothing else tomboyish about her. Her sleek body couldn't be hidden even under the gray sweatshirt and bib overalls. "Howdy, Mr. Bolan."

"Belinda's from New Jersey," Shawnee explained, "so all that 'howdy' and 'shucks' stuff is just her rap. She wants to be a country singer."

Belinda's smile widened. "When in Rome, right?"

Shawnee continued. "This is Lynn Booker. Our legal adviser."

"Not much of a job since everything we do is illegal," Lynn said, looking straight at Bolan. Her Eurasian features were accented by the shadows in the dimly lit room. She was short, barely five feet, with straight, shiny black hair chopped off at the shoulders. The angled eyes and thin mouth only enhanced her beauty.

"Vietnamese?" Bolan asked.

"Half," Lynn said with no trace of accent. "GI father, Vietnamese mother. They knew each other for one night, if that long. My mother disappeared when I was thirteen. I was adopted by Gerald and Martha Booker of St. Petersburg, Florida. Got my law degree and passed the bar exam last year." Her tone was clipped, businesslike.

"Last and least," Shawnee said, "Rita St. Clair. Big-bucks Boston family. Banking or something."

"Insurance," Rita said.

"Whatever. Anyway, Rita chucks the whole debutante/Vassar/married-to-an-ambassador crap to become—get this—a cop."

Bolan's jaw flexed.

"Relax," Rita told Bolan, "I'm not a cop now. Not that I ever really was one. After all my Academy training in Boston, I get this job in Coolidge, Georgia. Five-person police department. In Boston I'd dragged bodies out of the river, been shot at, even stabbed by some junkie with a hunk of mirror. Here they make me a meter maid. Fine, I'm willing to pay my dues like anyone else. But every time there's a promotion, they give it to one of the men, guys with less experience, less seniority. I'd gone into police work because I wanted to make a difference, and I sought out a small town so I could at least *see* the difference. But it never happened. So I quit."

"Well, not completely quit," Shawnee said, a huge grin arcing her lips. "She joined with us."

"Us?" Bolan said. "Who's us?"

"Us," Shawnee said, gesturing with her hand to include the four women. "We're the Savannah Swingsaw. And we, Mack Bolan, are gonna help you bust your friend out of jail."

11

The man with one blue and one brown eye walked among the dusty antiques, some authentic, some merely old junk. He picked up various objects—rusting swords, musty hats, carved ivory chess pieces—examined them carefully, then replaced them. Never making a sound.

The shop owner, Giles Tandy, a native Atlantan whose father had started the store and tried to teach its intricacies to his unwilling son, had inherited the business two years before, following his father's third heart attack. By that time, Giles had already been an unsuccessful insurance salesman, unsuccessful swimming pool salesman and unsuccessful truck salesman.

Since his father had always been successful, Giles decided to try his hand at Daddy's antique business. His mother, who helped out part-time, tried to argue with him to maintain the same business integrity as his father, but Giles was indifferent to integrity. He added shoddy garage-sale crap to the quality items his father had carefully purchased, making the store what it was today. A mixture of superb antiques and castaway junk. He thought the dust added an air of authenticity.

"Help you, sir?" he said to the man with one blue eye and one brown eye. Hadn't even noticed the stranger sneaking around back here so damn quiet. He looked at the man's expensive suit, the quiet manner, figured him for some kind of banker or accountant and turned on the charm. "We got the finest antiques this side of the Mississippi, sir. Indeed, the best on either side."

The man continued to browse, ignoring Giles. On the other side of the store an elderly lady was pawing through the cheap bric-a-brac. At most, she'd spend ten dollars. He decided to stay with the money man.

Giles shivered slightly when he looked at the man's face. His eyes were spooky, not just because of the different colors, but just the way they looked at Giles, as if he wasn't there. As if Giles was a bug and he was trying to decide whether or not to squash him. Still, the man obviously had money. The watch and ring were gold.

Giles was having trouble maintaining his smile while the tall thin man ignored him. The old lady had left, leaving just the two of them in the store.

The browser ran his hand along one of the music boxes on the glass showcase that Giles had bought from a bankrupt bakery. He watched the fingers and shuddered. They were long and skinny, like the legs of a spider.

"Now that's a hell of a choice, sir," Giles said enthusiastically. "That there music box comes out of France, made around 1683. A present from the French to, uh, Spain."

The thin tall man turned his head and stared at Giles. It was like being slapped in the face. Giles swallowed nervously.

"You are a liar, sir," the man said. His voice was soft, almost a whisper. His English was precise yet without tone, not American, yet having no identifiable accent. "The music box was not invented until about 1770, probably in Switzerland. Second, in 1683, France and Spain were at war." The man turned away and continued through the store, examining other items.

Giles felt sweat trickle behind his ears. Hell, he'd been called a liar before, but never with such a menacing, threatening tone. Okay, so he'd made up a date and some history for the customer. He did it all the time. Was that such a crime?

"Anything in particular you're looking for, sir?"

The man looked up again. He smiled, his teeth small even squares. "Branding irons."

Damn nuisance, Giles thought, wondering what the guy wanted with a branding iron. But then he smiled because he remembered they actually did have a couple of irons his father had bought from a ranch that had been plowed under into an eighteen-hole golf course. "Er, yes, we've got branding irons. All kinds. Just take me a minute."

Giles went into the back, rummaged through one of the storage lockers and returned to the display area with three rusty branding irons. "Quite a history here," he started to say, but stopped abruptly when the man's eyes met his with an unspoken warning.

The three branding irons looked completely different. One had a long handle with a reversed *K* on one end. The *K* had little upward angles at the bottom, like feet. The second iron was much shorter, with an ornate heart around the letter *N*. The third iron merely had a curve or hook at the end, no symbol.

Giles thought maybe the third one had lost its branding symbol. "I'm sure I can find the rest of it out back," he offered. "Just take me a second."

The man's thin mouth curved downward in distaste. "You are not only a liar, but also a fool."

"Now look here, mister—"

The man raised the third branding iron and pressed it against Giles's forehead. Though the metal was cold, Giles winced as if it was glowing red. Still, he didn't dare move.

"You see," the man explained patiently, "originally in this country, brands were used chiefly to punish humans. Runaway slaves, indentured servants who tried to escape. Not until the expansion into the West did branding cattle become common."

"Well, uh. . . ." Giles swallowed.

"The brand—" he pressed it harder against Giles's forehead, cutting into the skin "—called a running iron, was used to draw a brand on a hide, rather than just stamp it on like these others. It was favored by cattle rustlers because it allowed them to change brands so easily. This branding iron has been outlawed in several states." He lowered the iron, stroked the metal.

Giles took a deep breath. "Oh."

"How much?" the man asked.

"Sir?"

"For the branding irons. All three."

"Well," Giles drawled, figuring in his head, "lots of history here. Cattle rustlers and all. Worth a lot of money."

The man with one blue eye and one brown eye opened his wallet, pulled out two crisp hundred-dollar bills, laid them on the counter, picked up the irons and walked toward the door.

Though he figured they might be worth more, something told Giles not to argue this one time. He rubbed the indentation on his forehead where the man had ground the branding iron.

As he reached the front door, the man glanced at his watch, turned to Giles and asked, "Pay phone?"

Giles pointed. "Half a block down, next to the grocery store."

Outside in the early morning sun, Zavlin blinked his sensitive eyes and quickly put his sunglasses on. He glanced at his watch again. Still a few minutes before he was due to call in. He was in a good mood, having picked up three additional items for his collection of Western memorabilia. He had perhaps the largest collection of branding irons in the world.

On more than one occasion, he'd had the opportunity to actually use his irons, firing them up over coals until they glowed a fierce orange. Then pressing them against the skin of a yelping man, woman or child from whom he had requested information.

Eventually, they all spoke, begged to answer his questions. There was nothing like the stench of sizzling flesh to persuade a stubborn tongue.

Zavlin found the public telephone, inserted his coins and began dialing. The voice at the other end was crisp, formal.

"Identify, please."

"The Gamesman."

"One moment."

The line crackled with static for a few seconds. Then another voice spoke.

"Gamesman?"

"Yes," Zavlin answered. "I am in position."

"Strategy change. Your opponent has altered his defense."

"What do you mean?" Zavlin demanded.

His control sighed. "A prisoner escaped last night."

"Who?"

"No one to concern us. Someone named Damon Blue."

"Did you run a check?"

"Of course, Gamesman." The voice was insulted. "Petty criminal. No relationship to your assignment."

"What is the current status?"

"Security increased. Lock-down throughout. Some prisoners transferred."

"The pawn?"

"He remains. I have some contacts that I can pressure to make sure."

"No."

"What?"

"No," Zavlin repeated, his voice whipping through the wire like an icy wind. "In fact, make certain he is transferred, it does not matter where. Just find out when the transfer will take place. While he is on his way, that is when I shall strike."

"But the original plan, the one already approved...."

"Impossible. This Damon Blue has ruined that now. They will be alerted inside. I would have to wait another week for security to ease."

"That would be too late."

"Exactly."

There was a long pause as Zavlin's control went through the motions of making a decision. Zavlin waited patiently, knowing there was only one way to decide, that this pause was only a matter of saving face. A show of false power.

"Yes, Gamesman. Play as you see fit."

Zavlin chuckled into the phone, allowing his control to hear him as he hung up. He hurried back to his hotel room to prepare. Control would have the information as to when Dodge Reed would be transferred, undoubtedly this very day.

By tonight, the boy would be dead.

12

"We're not feminist vigilantes, Mack," Shawnee said.

"I didn't say that," Bolan said. The morning sun was bright through the kitchen curtains. The five of them were sitting around the table. Shawnee and Belinda were sipping coffee, Lynn and Rita were nibbling on peanut butter and crackers. Bolan dug with relish into the bacon-and-onions omelet Belinda had made for him.

"We're not a bunch of bimbos, for heaven's sake."

"I didn't say that, either."

"Like hell. We managed to break you out of jail but you don't think we're good enough to go along with you on this one. What kind of bullshit is that?"

The four women stared at him expectantly.

Bolan held up his fork. "Listen, I appreciate what you tried to do for me. But the mission's going to be a lot tougher. By now they've got extra security all around the place. They've probably even gone to a total lock-down, no one out of their cells for a few days."

"I can contact Lyle, find out for sure."

Bolan shook his head. "They won't allow any communication except with lawyers. That's procedure. By now they've also found the bodies of Rodeo and his bunch. That will only make things worse." Bolan scanned each one of their faces. "How *did* you break me out anyway?"

Shawnee smiled. "With a little help from one of the guards. For a lot of money."

"Does he know who I am?"

"Nope. I had to tell Lyle, though."

"I owe you," Bolan said.

"Damn right you do, fella," Shawnee said. "And this is where we get paid off. By going along."

"I can't risk getting you involved. It's not just the cops I'm worried about. There are other factors involved. Professional killers."

"The Mob? Hell, we've dealt with them before. Remember, we're the Savannah Swingsaw."

"This isn't the Mob. This guy makes the Mafia look like a kindergarten class on a nature stroll."

Shawnee flipped her long black hair over her shoulder. The sharp widow's peak at the top of her forehead emphasized her anger. She gestured with her head at the other women and they quickly filed out of the kitchen, closing the door behind them.

"We gotta talk serious, Mack," Shawnee said. "You've known me for a long time, but in a lotta ways you don't know me at all." She stood up, took her coffee cup to the stove, poured more coffee and leaned against the counter while drinking it. "You may think this Savannah Swingsaw stuff is hokey or juvenile, but we take it very seriously."

"Just what are you trying to accomplish?"

"That's funny coming from you."

Bolan chewed his omelet, waiting.

"We're trying to make the Mob so uncomfortable around Georgia that they'll move out. We do it, not by randomly killing them—we haven't killed anybody yet—but by exposing them to the harsh light of publicity. We bust in someplace and break the joint up, that gets press. We keep doing it, keep Clip Demoines's name in the papers, the public will demand some action or Demoines's bosses will insist he close up shop. Either way we win. What have you got to say to that?"

"A worthy goal."

"Damn right. Thing is, Mack, I started this operation, got the girls together, me and Rita training them. And you know what gave me the idea?"

"I think so, but I hope I'm wrong."

"You aren't. You did. Especially when I read you were dead. Funny thing, you and I were buddies back in Nam, attractive tough-guy GI and a dumpy nurse. We never had anything romantic going, but I loved you like a brother. When you came back and started your campaign against the Mob, I think I loved you even more."

Bolan nodded. He knew what she meant. They'd been pals at a time when friendship was more important than romance. The bonds made over in that hellground had been forged in a fire more intense than anywhere else. Those bonds could never be broken.

"But why start attacking the Mob, Shawnee? Did you have some personal run-in with them?"

Shawnee smiled. "No. Lynn Booker had. Her adopted parents used to manage an apartment house in Daytona. Turns out the government's Witness Protection Program had relocated one of their stoolies in this apartment house. Somehow the Mob found out and sent a couple of goons over to wipe the guy out. The Bookers saw them speeding away from the murder. Lynn's parents were all set to testify at the trial when their home was broken into one night while they were in bed. Lynn was away at college."

Shawnee paused, took a deep breath.

"They beat Mr. Booker, breaking his jaw, both arms. Mrs. Booker—she was fifty-seven then—was raped by both men, then beaten. They refused to testify. Lynn says her parents have never been able to live with not testifying, the shame of cowardice. That was worse on them than the beatings."

"The others?" Bolan asked.

"Oh, Rita's more like me. Idealistic, though you'd probably say naive. She's seen what they can do, but hasn't been touched directly by them. But she's fought more crime with me than when she was a real cop on that Mickey Mouse police force."

"What about Belinda? The singer."

Shawnee nodded. "Yeah, Belinda. A few years ago she and her boyfriend left Newark for Nashville. Trying to break into the country-music business. Scraped by on odd jobs for a year until finally getting a recording offer. Nothing major, but a start, a possibility. Along comes a so-called manager, tells them he's gonna take over their act, make them stars.

"Well, Belinda's fella, Tommy, was also their manager, so they refused. Belinda comes home from her waitress job two nights later, finds Tommy unconscious, a razor cut across his chin and a note saying it could just as easily have been his throat. They go to the cops, are told the 'manager' is Mob connected but there isn't much the cops can do. Next night Belinda comes home, Tommy's packed and gone to L.A. to try the rock business." She rinsed her cup out and placed it in the sink. "So that's the story of the Savannah Swingsaw. We've been busting up joints for the past few months, making it hot around here for Demoines and his boys."

Bolan shoved his empty plate away and looked up at Shawnee.

Her story had touched him in a way he hadn't expected. He'd heard plenty of stories of lives scarred or ruined by encounters with the Mob, and he'd known a few people who were angry enough to try and get revenge. Most of them cooled down when they realized what they were up against. Others went about it rashly and got themselves killed. But Shawnee wasn't motivated by revenge; she was doing this because she thought it was right. Simple as that.

"What's wrong?" she asked.

"I was thinking. I was just a soldier when this all started for me. And even then I was only reacting to what they'd done to my family. Pure revenge. What would have happened if my family hadn't ever come in contact with any of the Mob? Would I have come home from Nam just happy to have survived, get myself a regular job and occasionally shake my head when I read in the newspapers what the Mafia was up to now? This whole war of mine only started out of vengeance. But you,'' he said, standing and moving closer to her, his eyes boring into hers, "had the guts to risk everything just because it was the right thing to do.''

Shawnee placed her hand gently on his arm. Her usual husky voice was soft and tender. "Maybe that's how you started, Mack, but that isn't what's kept you going all these years, through all those risks. Okay, it started as a personal vendetta, but now it's bigger than that. It's a damn crusade.''

"Trouble with you,'' Bolan said, grinning, "is you know too much.''

"Sometimes,'' she said, "I don't know when to shut up.'' And suddenly she stepped up to Bolan and wrapped her arms around his waist. Her face tilted up toward his and he lowered his lips to hers.

It felt so natural to him. They'd hugged many times before, giving friendly pecks on the cheek as they came and went. But this was different, more than friendly. Her body was hard and sinewy, sexy and insistent as she pressed against him and his arms pulled her even closer.

For a moment, a vision of April Rose flickered through his mind. She was standing as she always stood, an expression of defiance mixed with concern on her delicate features. She was scolding him, but smiling at the same time.

Maybe, Bolan thought, it was April's love that

had kept him from becoming *too* hard, too much like their enemies. Revenge was a powerful fuel, sure, but it was dangerous. It could destroy the very engine it was fueling. April had kept that from happening to Bolan. Yeah, he missed her. Always would. But he couldn't deny certain feelings he had for Shawnee. Not brotherly feelings anymore.

"You think this kiss will make me change my mind?" Bolan said when they parted.

"About what?" she said.

He grinned. "Okay, I'm going to use you and your Savannah Swingsaw. Not because of anything that's happened between us, but because I have an idea."

"All right!" Rita cheered as she and the other women burst into the kitchen.

Bolan rolled his eyes to the ceiling. Obviously they'd been crouched just on the other side of the door, listening.

Then his face became grim. "You won't be so happy once you hear the plan."

13

"What the hell happened? There's a pile of dead bodies lying around the morgue with toe tags that might as well read 'courtesy of Mack Bolan.' I show up at the jail as your attorney to have a meeting and find out you've busted out of the place. And without Dodge Reed, dammit. Now you tell me you've put together an assault squad made up of four women?"

Bolan spoke into the phone. "That about covers it."

Hal Brognola sighed.

Bolan heard a crunching sound. His friend was chewing those tablets again.

"Okay, Mack, okay. You need some backup. Fine. Just tell me what's going down and where, I'll be there. I still know how to use a gun."

"Can't do it, pal," Bolan said. "If this doesn't go down right, we'll still need someone alive to stop Zavlin and find out what Dodge Reed knows. Besides, these women know what they're doing. I trust them."

"Then I do, too." There was a wistful tone in the Fed's voice, a disappointment that he wasn't going along. Maybe riding that desk really was getting to him. Maybe he did need to see some action.

"Okay, Hal. I need some information on Reed. What's his status in the jail?"

"Last time I checked was about an hour ago. They were planning on moving about two dozen inmates to different prisons. He was one of them."

"That's odd," Bolan said, staring out through the scratched phone-booth door. Shawnee was at the self-service pump filling her battered old Toyota. She waved at him and he smiled.

"Why odd?"

"They'd be moving some of the hardcore guys out, the real bad ones, but not a new fish like Reed."

"Think Zavlin's behind the move?"

"Think it gets dark at night?"

"Right. I'll have the transfer order rescinded. We'll keep him at Fulton."

"No," Bolan said. "Let him go."

"Why? Zavlin's bound to hit him in transit."

"Not if we get to him first."

Hal Brognola paused. "What do you need?"

"Reed's transit schedule. Times, route, that sort of thing."

"Weapons?"

"Seems the Savannah Swingsaw comes prearmed. We're okay there."

"It'll take me a minute to get the information. Can you hold on?"

"Yeah," Bolan said. He stared through the glass at Shawnee. There was a sense of power beneath her tenderness, a feeling of strength that was more than physical.

Brognola came back on the phone with a grumble.

"What do you want first, the bad news or the bad news?"

"Go on."

"Zavlin's still not been sighted, but three KGB agents attached to the Soviet embassy as cultural officers have been spotted here. You've got to figure they're going to help Zavlin in the assassination."

"He's not taking any chances. Whatever Reed knows, it must be damned important."

"Yeah, well, it gets worse. Reed's van is gassed and waiting right now. He's being transported with four other prisoners, a driver and a guard. They leave within the next twenty minutes."

"Not much time."

"There's an understatement. At least the route has possibilities." He outlined the streets for Bolan.

"Thanks, guy," Bolan said. "Gotta run."

"Good luck, Mack. And, hey, thank the Savannah Swingsaw for me. I don't want to lay any patriotic rap on them, but we appreciate what they're doing. Maybe we can work out some kind of immunity deal on their raids."

"I'll tell them," Bolan said. "But they'd have helped me, anyway." Bolan hung up.

Shawnee pulled the Toyota up to the phone booth with a screech, popping the passenger door open. Bolan climbed in.

"I've got the route and the time schedule."

She whistled, impressed. "That's some phone pal you've got there, Mack. How'd an outlaw like you get to know guys like that?"

"Who said it was a guy?"

She laughed. "Touché. Caught in my own sexist trap. Okay. I'll shut up and drive. Not much farther," she said, urging the gas pedal to the floor.

A few minutes later she yanked the car to the curb at an awkward angle and the two of them dashed up the stairs to the second floor of Shawnee's apartment.

The others were waiting and ready.

The weapons were spread out on the living-room floor on a canvas tarp.

Bolan stooped beside the cache, examining the arsenal.

"We brought most everything back from the hideout as you asked," Rita St. Clair said.

Bolan immediately picked up the prize of the collection, a Krico Super Sniper, the rifle long favored by police in Europe for picking off bad guys at five hundred meters. To the novice it looked like just another bolt-action rifle. It wasn't. The barrel was heavy, straight-tapered. Rifling was deep, with a fast twist that gave the bullet high rotational velocity for gyroscopic stabilization. The barrel was free-floating in its walnut stock, removing any pressure spots inside that could deflect the bullet as the barrel produces its sinusoidal wave whip on firing. Topping it off was a Beeman R66 scope.

"Nice," Bolan said, looking up at Rita.

She smiled. "I still have some friends from the force. Get me a few specialty items."

Bolan studied her a moment. Tall, poised, hair light brown with an almost reddish tint. Her clothes were no more expensive or fancy than the other women's—black denim pants, blue sweater, black jersey vest—but she wore them with the easy grace of a model. She looked confident, sure of herself. Some of that came from her aristocratic background, no doubt, but a lot of it had been earned out on the streets as a cop. And in the department as a woman.

Bolan picked through the rest of the guns. A Remington Model 870 shotgun; an H&K 93 with retracting stock, bipod, scope and mount; a Stevens Model 520 shotgun, two Star Model PD .45s, and two S&W Model 586 .357s with eight-inch barrels. Better than he'd hoped for.

"Well?" Shawnee asked.

"It'll do." Bolan snatched up the black pants and black turtleneck sweater they'd bought for him on their way back from retrieving the guns. "I'll change and we'll hit the road."

Lynn Booker stood up from the sofa, drinking from a can of cola. "Belinda wants to see you first. In the kitchen."

Bolan tucked his clothes under his arm and marched to the kitchen. The door was closed. When he entered, the radio was playing classical music. Belinda was sitting at the kitchen table humming along. Lined up on the table were a dozen grenades. They were standard Army olive with yellow lettering that said Hand Grenades, Frag M26, Comp B.

"This what they taught you in home ec?" Bolan said.

Belinda laughed, twisting a lock of her short blond hair between her fingers. "The way to a man's heart and all that. Of course, these babies will remove that heart first.'' There was no phony country twang in her voice now, just pure New Jersey.

Bolan picked up one of the grenades.

''Where'd you get these?'' he asked. ''They're Army.''

''We took 'em from one of Demoines's places we raided. Guess he stole them. Can you use them?''

Bolan looked at Belinda, sitting there, calmly discussing grenades. With those pale green eyes it was hard to believe she was part of the same Savannah Swingsaw that had been terrorizing the local Mafia kingpin, Clip Demoines. Except that Shawnee had already told him Belinda's specialty was handling the chain saw. Cut through a roulette table faster than a hot knife through butter.

''Yeah,'' Bolan replied. ''They won't go to waste. Now get out of here and let me change. We leave in two minutes.''

She smiled, ducked out of the room.

Bolan changed into the dark clothes and was back in the living room in less than a minute. ''Who are the best shots?''

''Rita's the best,'' Shawnee said. ''Then me.''

''Then me,'' Lynn said. She stood in the middle of the room, the can of cola in one hand, the H&K 93 in the other.

Bolan looked at her pretty Vietnamese features and flashed back for a moment to Nam. He shook it off just as quickly. ''Okay, that means Belinda waits for us at your safe house out in the country. Once we've snatched Dodge Reed, we'll be coming straight there, so have the second car ready and waiting. Also, the cash and change of clothes for everyone.''

"Check," Belinda said.

"Good. Now, anybody got something we can carry those grenades in?"

Shawnee snapped her fingers. "My bike pack. It's small, but they'll fit." She dashed down the hall into the bedroom and brought it back to Bolan. It was dark blue with a red reflector sewn onto the back. Bolan ripped the reflector off, loaded the grenades and swung the pack onto his back. He grabbed one of the S&W Model 586 .357s and stuck it in his pants under his sweater. He pocketed a box of shells.

Shawnee grabbed the other .357 as well as the Remington Model 870 shotgun. Rita took the Krico Super Sniper. They left the Stevens shotgun and the .45s for Belinda to take back to the cabin.

The women looked tense, like a sports team right before a big game. Only more so.

"Relax," Bolan said, leading them out the door. "What's one more kidnapping among friends?"

14

"What's this all about?" Lyle Carrew asked the guard who was unlocking his cell.

"They wanna talk to you. That's all they tole me."

Carrew wheeled out of the cell and started down the walk ahead of the guard. The guard knew better than to try to push the chair for Carrew, even down those four tricky stairs at the end. The guy let it be known he did things for himself, so that's the way it would be.

They arrived at the warden's office ten minutes later. The warden's secretary was close to seventy-five now, and looked at every prisoner, no matter his crime, with the same scolding expression, as if they were naughty boys up to no good.

"Go ahead in," she told Carrew. "And you behave yourself. Warden left instructions that everyone cooperate fully with that man in there. Governor's office and all."

"Okay, Mrs. Simpson," the black inmate said, opening the door and wheeling into the warden's office.

The man behind the warden's desk was not the warden, just as Mrs. Simpson had indicated. He was a tall thin man in a cheap, ill-fitting suit. Although he looked to be in his late thirties, his hair was pure white. The dark brown eyes contrasted with the white hair and fair skin to give him an intense look. He sucked on a pipe, puffing bitter smoke into the air as Carrew rolled closer.

"Come in, Mr. Carrew." He spoke with a lavish Southern accent, smiling around the stem of his pipe. " 'Preciate your coming in here and talking with me like this."

"What do you want, Colonel Sanders?"

The man looked confused for a moment, then chuckled. "Oh, yes, Colonel Sanders. The white hair. Very funny." He chuckled again. " I'm Jacob Frye from the governor's office, Mr. Carrew. The governor's a little concerned about what's gone on here in the past twenty-four hours. Four prisoners murdered, one guard with his head bashed in who claims he didn't see nothin'. Another prisoner escapes." He spread his hands as if hopelessly confused. "What am I to think?"

"Beats me."

"Damon Blue was your cell mate."

"True."

"He had a run-in with one of the murdered prisoners, Bertrand Stovell, also called Rodeo. Over another prisoner, uh. . . ." He checked the open file folder on the desk. "Some kid, Dodge Reed."

"I don't know anything about that."

"You were there in the yard when it happened."

Carrew shrugged. "Big yard."

The man stood up, sighed with frustration. "The

governor doesn't want some kind of Attica thing going on down here, not this close to election. We've had enough bad publicity about our prison system. Now if there are problems, let's hear about them. Let's talk reforms. If it's a racial thing, let's rap, work out the details. Just tell me what you know about Damon Blue. Who helped him escape?''

Carrew laughed. '' 'Let's rap?' Where you been, man, this is the eighties. You've been reading outdated books about the jargon of black Americans. Can you dig it, bro?''

The man shook his head sternly, picking at a loose thread on his jacket sleeve. ''I'm sorry if you find my concern amusing, Mr. Carrew. Most of the men in here don't have the luxury of being able to get out to a comfortable university professorship. A university funded, I might point out, by state money. Money controlled to some degree by the governor.''

''Are you threatening to have me fired, Mr. Frye?''

The man laughed softly, circling around the desk, walking behind Carrew's wheelchair. Carrew didn't bother turning around to look at the white-haired man. ''No, no, Mr. Carrew. The governor never makes threats. It was merely a civics lesson, nothing more, I assure you.'' A moment of silence as Carrew felt the man's presence directly behind him. ''The governor believes much more in the carrot than the stick.''

''Ah, a bribe.''

''An offering. One hand washing the other. Charges dropped, record cleared.''

"And you want what?"

"Just information."

"About Damon Blue."

"Yes. And his relationship with Dodge Reed."

Carrew shook his head. "I don't know anything. He was my cell mate for a couple days. Kept to himself."

"That's all?" he said, stepping around to face Carrew, those brown eyes burning under the white hair. "That's all you intend to tell me?"

"That's all," Carrew said.

The man looked at his watch, sighed again. "I believe you, Mr. Carrew. And it's getting too late to keep trying."

There was something in the man's voice that startled Carrew. The rich Southern accent was gone, the tone flat, the speech precise. He was picking at the thread on his sleeve button again when Carrew saw the button pop off and thread emerge from the sleeve into a foot-long wire with a button on the other end. Suddenly the tall man was behind him, the metal strand looped around his neck.

The handicapped black tried to get his hand up to protect his throat, but the tall man was too fast. The wire pinned the tip of Carrew's middle finger against his own throat as the garrote bit deep into the nail. He could feel his pulse thrashing wildly in his neck. He dropped his free hand to grope for the shank hidden in his chair. But the pressure of the tightening wire kept him off balance.

He felt the wire sawing through his finger, slicing into the sides of his neck. Finally, in a burst of strength from the tall man, the thin wire severed the tip of the finger, freeing Carrew's hand, but allowing the wire to sink into his throat. He grabbed at the wire, fingernails clawing to get at it.

He stretched his hands back, clamped them around the tall man's wrists, trying to break the grip. He couldn't. His own strength was ebbing. He could feel the warm blood dripping down his throat as if he'd dribbled on himself while drinking coffee. His hands fell to his sides helpless. Long bony fingers grasped his chin and the back of his head and he knew what was coming next even as he felt the sudden pressure of hands pushing and pulling in opposite directions, heard his vertebrae cracking as his neck broke and he slumped into his wheelchair and into death.

Zavlin unwound the wire from Carrew's neck, stuffed it into his pocket.

He'd found out all he could here. He figured his forged papers would be good for an hour before suspicions might arise. The hour was almost up. It had been a risk, but he had to make sure about this Damon Blue, be certain no one had learned anything from Dodge Reed.

The black man, Carrew, knew something, but it would have taken too long to force him to talk. He was too tough. Better to kill him, make sure he didn't tell anyone else whatever he found out.

Zavlin checked his watch again. He had almost ruined everything by his misuse of the black jargon. He was a master at accents, languages, dialects. But there were a few he still had trouble with, especially the black street talk. It changed too quickly, always adding new words, altering the meanings of existing ones.

He popped the contact lens out of his right eye. The tinted lens had changed the color from blue to brown, but he didn't like keeping it in too long. It irritated his eye. He blinked rapidly and put it back in. Then he left the room, telling the ancient secretary and the guard outside the door that he wanted to get some documents from his car and would return. They weren't to disturb the prisoner, but if he attempted to make a phone call, they were to monitor it. The old crone seemed to get some pleasure from that possibility.

Ten minutes later, Zavlin was driving through Atlanta to meet the three KGB assassins he'd sent for. By now they should already be in position. The prison van carrying Dodge Reed was only a few minutes behind him. Just as he'd planned.

15

"So what's the plan, Mack?" Shawnee piloted her ancient Celica up the Northeast Expressway to Buford Boulevard, edging just past the speed limit, but not enough to alert any cops.

"The plan," Bolan said sternly, "is to do what I say, when I say. Understood?"

Shawnee swung her head around, the long dark hair whipping off her shoulders like striking snakes. Her eyes glowered. "No, damn it, not understood at all. You may be the famous Mack Bolan, but this is still my squad. The Savannah Swingsaw follows my orders. You want to discuss the details of the plan, fine. We're with you. You want to play leader, then we pass."

"These men are dangerous," Bolan persisted.

"Hey, Mack," Shawnee said with a sigh. "You may have kicked ass in every state of the union, but we've kicked some ass of our own. We know dangerous."

The Executioner decided she was right. They knew danger. But not the kind that came with men like Zavlin. He had no rules, no mercy. And he was trained in ways to kill that rivaled even the ancient cult of ninjas.

"Well?" she said, glancing from the road to his face with her piercing eyes. "What's it going to be?"

He looked over his shoulder to Lynn and Rita in the back seat. He knew their guns were hidden on the floor under a blanket, but the women were perched on the edge of the seat ready to grab them at a second's notice. They returned his gaze with unblinking stares.

Good, he thought. He could see they were a united front. That was important. It was just what he was trying to determine by his rough prodding and insults. See how much of a team they really were, how much leadership Shawnee had. The way all three of them were glaring at him now, he knew they could be counted on to stick together when things started to get bloody.

And they would.

"Okay," he said, spreading the map of Atlanta and surrounding areas on his lap. "You wanted to know the plan. Listen carefully."

They listened, their faces growing paler as he explained.

ZAVLIN REMOVED HIS SUNGLASSES, wincing from the harsh sunlight. His one brown eye and his one blue eye squinted immediately. He shaded them with one hand while using the other to unsnap the leather case around his neck and bring the binoculars up to his sensitive eyes.

Yes! There they were. His three KGB assistants were in perfect position. They crouched in the thick dogwood and pink azaleas, waiting for the van, their high-powered rifles clutched in experienced hands. They were very good.

Zavlin permitted himself a tiny premature smile of victory.

He carried the folding beach chair that he'd bought at the discount drugstore on the way here to just the right spot under a shady tree and sat down with a contented sigh. Might as well relax. What would happen next was as inevitable as snow in Moscow.

He peered through the binoculars again, adjusting the central focusing drive. His men were dressed in casual clothing: golf shirts, Bermuda shorts, dark socks, loafers. Just what a tourist might be wearing who got lost in the area.

Once they'd disposed of the guns, the only thing that might betray them were the identical calluses on the inside crooks of their trigger fingers. Thick pads from pulling triggers of hundreds of guns. Built up from years of irritating the skin, like oysters creating pearls from the nuisance of a single grain of sand. To each of those men, that callus was as valuable as a pearl.

He reached inside his shirt to fondle the gold-plated ornament hanging from the gold chain around his neck. The object puzzled the few who had seen it, guessing that perhaps it was some sort of shark's tooth, or the claw from a giant leopard.

It was a finger. The skeletal fragment of a finger. Supposedly the finger bone of the legendary American, Jim Bowie. Not just any finger, but his trigger finger, sliced off at the Alamo by one of Santa Anna's men. Not out of hate, but in tribute to his heroism.

The bony digit had been passed down through generations of this same Mexican military family until hard times had forced them to sell it to a private broker. Zavlin ran his fingertips along the gold plating he'd added. There was no way to authenticate this as Jim Bowie's, it could be any finger. He didn't care. He wanted it to be Bowie's, so it was. Certainly he'd paid enough money to the broker, who would know the dire consequences of cheating Zavlin, for it to be real.

Zavlin watched from the shade of his tree, able to see everything, observe his men take aim when the prison van came within range, and fire and keep firing until Dodge Reed was dead. As well as everyone else in the van.

And, should anything go wrong, he would be safely up here.

He swung his binoculars down the dirt road. A puff of dust rose and grew like the tail of a frightened cat. He couldn't make out what the vehicle was yet, but it had to be going to the new prison. That was the only place the road led to.

Not a prison yet. It hadn't been completed. But the walls were up and where they weren't, barbed wire had been strung. The dormitories hadn't been finished yet either, but the plumbing was working and they'd constructed rows of tents for the convicts to sleep in. Nothing unusual in that.

Zavlin had read of many prisons fighting overcrowding with small tent cities. And recent troubles at Fulton had convinced authorities to use the new prison a little early while they investigated the prison murders, defusing what they feared might be a race war.

A helpful, well-paid secretary, had managed to include Dodge Reed's name among those scheduled to be transferred. The amount of her bribe had been staggering, but it was money well spent, Zavlin thought. The whole KGB operation could be jeopardized if Dodge Reed told anyone what he knew. And that operation was too important to risk. Not when they were so close to striking what surely would be a crippling blow to the entire American society.

The vehicle wobbled closer, still engulfed in the cloud of dust, defying identification. Zavlin glanced down at his men. They scrambled to their positions and readied their rifles.

Zavlin could feel the familiar excitement as he pressed the binoculars back to his eyes, zeroing in on the approaching dust cloud. Public outcry had forced the location of this prison to be changed from the more populated areas to more rustic locales. Getting here had been the biggest challenge so far. But it was for the best. There would be no one to stop what was about to happen.

The plume of dust hugged the winding road, clinging to the bouncing vehicle like a coat of buzzing flies. Another half mile and it would be on the short straight road that Zavlin had determined was the best location for the ambush.

If only that stupid record-store manager had told

his boss about Dodge Reed first. But no, the manager, all of twenty-five and filled with self-importance over his recent promotion, had not only fired Reed, but had him *arrested*! It had all happened so quickly that by the time the boss had found out and informed his own KGB contacts, it was too late to drop the charges without arousing suspicion.

Both the manager and the boss would be dealt with later. After Dodge Reed had been eliminated.

The dust swirl swept around the final curve and hit the straight section of road. Zavlin adjusted his binoculars and smiled brightly.

The van.

And there, leaning against the window, was the morose young face of Dodge Reed.

The KGB assassin shifted his glasses to take in the whole van. The rush of dust would complicate an already difficult shot. His marksmen would have to stop the van first.

Just as the thought entered his mind, the sharp crack of a rifle shot echoed up to him and he saw the front left tire of the van explode. The rear of the van swung out, skidding across the dirt road as the driver wrestled with the steering wheel. Then the glass on the driver's side shattered and the driver's head collapsed into red mush. He was flung out of his seat and the van, uncontrolled, spun to a halt.

The six prisoners, each handcuffed to his seat, yelled and hollered as they ducked down under the windows, only their cuffed wrists showing. The remaining guard had his gun drawn and was hunched down, peering out the shattered window for a target.

Only a tiny sliver of his head was visible. But that was enough.

One of the KGB assassins tightened his callous finger around his trigger and the top of the guard's head flew off like a soggy red toupee. The prisoners hollered even louder. They were trapped, without weapons, bound to their seats.

Now all Zavlin's men had to do was walk in and mop up. A bullet in the head of each man, three in Dodge Reed's head. Just to make sure. He watched them stalking toward the disabled van, their guns ready.

Very good, Zavlin thought, lowering the binoculars.

A volley of shots startled him and he raised his binoculars.

The van was still sitting there, unmoving, the prisoners yelling for help.

He aimed the binoculars at his men just as another fusillade boomed through the valley. One of his KGB hit men spun, fired a shot into the brush. A shotgun blast ruffled dogwood leaves as the pellets brushed aside everything in their path, then punched through the KGB agent's chest like an iron fist. The agent was jerked off his feet as he flew backward into the azaleas.

Zavlin was on his feet, the binoculars screwed to his eyes.

BOLAN SHOULDERED HIS WAY through the dogwood, dropped to one knee and squeezed off two rounds from his S&W .357. It was a little barrel-heavy, but that heaviness allowed full development of gas pressure behind the bullet. The double-action squeeze was absorbed by the tension of the mainspring inside the grip.

The bullets shredded some leaves but otherwise missed the two fleeing assassins. Bolan hadn't really expected to hit them. They were moving too fast and with too much skill. The KGB trained its field agents as if they were Olympic athletes. Some of them were.

Shawnee appeared at Bolan's side. "One down."

"Nice shot."

"You kidding? With this thing I'd have to be blindfolded to miss."

He didn't look at her, but sensed her nervousness. Not from what was ahead, but from what she'd just done. For all her time in Vietnam, she'd never hurt anyone before. She'd been a nurse, healing wounds, cursing the weapons that did this kind of damage. Sure, lately she'd been busting down some Mafia doors and chopping the joints up. But all she'd needed to do then was point her gun, threaten.

Now she was pulling the trigger.

And a man's chest had burst out his back.

He felt her shivering next to him, trying hard to tough it out, not let him know how she felt. But he knew.

Despite the years of violence, the trail of corpses, Bolan still remembered that first body, the look of surprise on that Cong sniper's face as Bolan's bullet plowed into his skull. It took a while to get over that.

But Shawnee didn't say anything. She hunkered next to the Executioner and waved for Rita and

Lynn. The two women ran up and knelt next to Bolan and Shawnee.

They'd been told to follow behind Bolan and Shawnee, so their path must have brought them to the dead KGB agent Shawnee had killed. Rita looked at the shotgun, then at Shawnee. Lynn, the most reserved of the women, nevertheless touched a comforting hand to Shawnee's shoulder, then withdrew it. Nothing was said among the women, but Bolan could sense a feeling of support, of unity. One he'd experienced many times in Nam and again with his men at Stony Man Farm.

"Rita, you and Lynn stay here and keep those two goons pinned down. If you hit them, fine, but our main priority is getting Dodge Reed free." Bolan checked his watch. "Give Shawnee and me five minutes to get to the van, release Reed and be on our way back to the car. Once the time is up, drop back and head for the car yourself. It'll take them a while to decide whether or not it's safe to follow us."

"Okay," Rita St. Clair said. "But with this baby—" she hefted her Krico Super Sniper "—I should be able to do a little more damage than just pin them down."

Lynn tapped her watch. "Five minutes. Go."

Bolan led Shawnee through the underbrush to the road. Behind them Lynn and Rita were peppering the hillside with a hard rain.

A few shots were being returned from the KGB agents and Shawnee stopped to make sure Lynn and Rita were okay.

"Come on," Bolan ordered. "As long as they stay under cover, they'll be fine."

Shawnee hesitated, but then ran after Bolan as they dashed for the van.

Bolan reached it first. He stepped into the vehicle, climbing over the bodies of the guards and ignoring the pleading of the men begging to be set free. Kneeling on the floor, he kept watch out the window while Shawnee checked the two guards. Bolan knew what she'd find, but he also knew she needed to try.

"Dead," she finally said. "Both of them."

Bolan nodded, started searching the bodies for the keys to the handcuffs. The prisoners were yanking and jerking at their cuffs, trying to dislodge the whole seat.

"It's you," Dodge Reed said as Bolan approached him with the key.

"Yeah, kid. You're coming with me."

"What's going on here?"

Bolan gave him a cold stare. "Don't you know?"

Reed shook his head. "Honestly, I don't know what you want."

Bolan paused. What if the kid was telling the truth? Then why was Zavlin trying to kill him? Either Reed was lying, or he knew something that he didn't know was important.

It didn't matter. Reed knew something. Something the KGB was willing to kill him for. Bolan had to know what that was. He jammed one of the keys into the cuff lock and turned. Nothing. He tried another key. And another.

"Hey, Blue," one of the prisoners yelled. "I know you, man. I seen you in Fulton. C'mon, man. Give us the keys."

"Give us the keys, Blue," another man demanded. Others chorused in their agreement.

Bolan ignored them, trying keys until he finally sprang Reed's lock. The kid seemed dazed, unable to move. He just sat on the floor in a stupor. Bolan grabbed him by the arm and yanked him to his feet. "Let's go!"

Reed stumbled after him.

As they headed for the front door of the van, uncuffed arms reached out and ensnared both Bolan and Reed. Bolan felt them grabbing at his arms and legs, trying to pull him down so they could get the keys. He used the eight-inch barrel of his .357 to smash fingers and hands, kicking his way free from the groping wall of arms. He pulled Reed after him, stopping to hammer the wrist of one stubborn prisoner who had hold of Reed's hair.

"They'll kill us, man!" one of the convicts whined to Bolan.

"No, they won't," Bolan assured him. "Once we're gone, their interest in you will be gone too. When you guys don't show up at the prison within the next ten minutes, they'll be sending a few squad cars after you. If you were free, they might think you had something to do with killing those guards. That would make you an accessory."

"Big fucking deal," one of them snapped. But the others, realizing that a manhunt for escaped cons involved in killing guards could result in their getting shot on sight, decided maybe it wasn't such a good idea to get out.

Bolan didn't care what they thought. He shoved Reed out of the van, nudged Shawnee to follow and brought up the rear. They ran for Shawnee's Celica, hidden under brush farther down the road.

ZAVLIN'S EYES HURT from pressing the binoculars so tightly against his face. But he couldn't stop. Not now. Not while he watched his men pinned down under a barrage of fire in a vulnerable location. Not while the man in black and the athletic woman stole Dodge Reed away.

He focused on the man in black, on the long square jaw that jutted out like the prow of some battleship. And those dark, menacing eyes, glowing with concentration as he ran, guiding the woman and Reed. Those were the eyes of a professional.

Zavlin kept the binoculars aimed at the man in black, studying him as a hunter studies a new prey, until the dark-clad figure disappeared into the brush.

Zavlin swung the binoculars back to his two men. Their position was undefendable. They were lucky that the two women didn't stalk after them, were satisfied with merely keeping them immobile.

Then one of Zavlin's men, obviously frustrated, began to move. His comrade tried to stop him, but he shook off the restraining hand and crawled belly-first from behind the brush. What's he doing, Zavlin wondered, running one hand through his white hair.

Now the two women were beginning to move. The Oriental looked at her watch and shouted something to her tall companion with the wicked-looking sniper rifle. The tall woman nodded and the two of them started in the same direction as the man in black.

Zavlin's angry assassin was gaining some high ground, climbing up to a clump of trees, shinnying up the trunk to a thick branch and taking aim with his rifle.

A shot thunderclapped in the valley.

Zavlin swung the binoculars around just in time to see the short Oriental woman spin around and tumble into the brush. The tall woman with the reddish hair immediately dropped to her knee, snapped the rifle to her shoulder, surveyed the hillside with her scope and triggered a round.

The agent in the tree returned fire. His bullet kicked up dirt three feet to the left of the woman. But she didn't move. She methodically adjusted her scope, aimed again and squeezed the trigger.

No return fire.

Zavlin whipped the binoculars around again, saw his man hanging at an awkward angle from the tree branch, the leg he'd wedged between branches for support now keeping him from falling. The front of his shirt was sopping with blood. There was a hole in his chest that looked as if a giant bird had been pecking at his heart.

The tall woman was helping the Oriental woman to her feet. Zavlin watched as she tore a strip of material from her blouse and wrapped it around the wounded woman's arm. Minor damage. They started off again, following the man in black.

Zavlin searched for his remaining agent, still

hunched in the brush, waiting. He alone had done the right thing, waiting until the firing stopped before making any move.

The white-haired killer got up from his folding chair and picked up the SIG PE-57 assault rifle he'd leaned against the shady tree. Squinting to protect his sensitive eyes from the sun, he chambered a 7.55mm Swiss cartridge, braced the stock against his shoulder and screwed his right eye to the scope. He tightened his hand around the black rubberlike pistol grip, and focused on his target.

He squeezed the trigger.

Through the scope he watched the shocked expression on his own KGB agent's face as his chest erupted in a sudden red mist. The man's thick Russian features stretched thin and rubbery from screaming, then went flaccid as his body flopped into the brush.

A shame, Zavlin thought, but necessary. The others were out of range, so there was nothing he could do about them. But he couldn't take a chance of his own man being caught by American authorities. Nor did he want him to tell KGB officials what had happened. It would reflect badly on Zavlin that some American agent had outguessed the KGB's top assassin, beating him to the target.

No. Zavlin would take care of the matter himself. He would find out more about Dodge Reed and the man in prison who had befriended him, Damon Blue. In the meantime, he would think about the man in black. Replay the humiliation he suffered today at that man's hands. And think of how he would kill him next time they met.

16

"I don't know anything. I swear!"

"Think harder," Bolan said.

Dodge Reed shook his head. "I don't know what you want."

"I want to know what information you have. The kind the KGB would be interested in."

"I don't have any information. Not for the KGB or anyone else."

Bolan blew an exasperated sigh and stamped harder on the gas pedal. The Toyota zipped around another curb on the way to the secluded cabin. Next to Bolan sat Dodge Reed, nervous, fidgeting with a loose piece of paper sticking out of the glove compartment. In the back seat, Rita kept watch out the rear window while Shawnee practiced her nursing on Lynn's arm.

"How is she?" Bolan asked Shawnee, watching her in the rearview mirror.

"Not too bad. Some blood loss, but nothing serious."

"That's easy for you to say," Lynn deadpanned.

Shawnee smiled. "I thought you Orientals are supposed to be strong silent types. No complaints. You lose face or something."

"Hey, losing face is one thing, but losing six inches of skin and half a pint of blood, even we Asians draw the line there."

Bolan watched Shawnee finish taping the bandage around Lynn's forearm. Some blood was already seeping through, but Shawnee had done a first-rate job and the bleeding would stop soon. He turned his attention back to Dodge Reed.

"Listen, son. By now you must know we saved you from the people who killed the guards back there."

"Maybe," Reed said, "but maybe you got the wrong guy. There were a bunch of other fellas in that van. Maybe you want one of them."

Bolan caught a glimpse of Shawnee's expression in the mirror. She looked doubtful, as though she wondered if maybe the kid was right, and he had made a mistake. The thing was, Dodge Reed was convincing. Bolan tended to believe him. But the KGB didn't make mistakes like that. If they wanted him dead, he knew something, something very important. Even if he didn't know that he knew.

"Let's take it from the top, kid."

Dodge Reed groaned. "Listen, Mr. Blue, I wanna help, I truly do. I appreciate you getting me away from those assassins and all, and if I knew what you wanted, I'd surely tell you. Out of sheer gratitude."

"Turn left up here," Shawnee interrupted.

"Where?"

She reached her arm over his shoulder and pointed to a narrow dirt road almost hidden by brush. It was an unmarked route that looked as if it had been hacked out of the brush with a butter knife. Branches scraped along the sides of the car as Bolan geared down to negotiate the trail.

"Go on, kid," Bolan said to Reed.

"Like I said, I'd tell you anything you wanted to know. But I honestly think you got the wrong guy. I'm just some college student studying computers at night and working in a record store during the day."

"In jail for embezzlement," Bolan reminded him.

"A mistake. Honest. I don't know why they got so damned upset. Sure I used their computer when I shouldn't have. But I had all this homework to do from my computer science class, and it was during my lunchtime anyway and the computer wasn't being used. I was just experimenting with this program I had to write. I dunno, it was weird."

"How so?"

"Well, first of all, I had to use their system disk. I didn't want to screw it up, so I just made a copy of their system disk and used that to work on my own program. I was having trouble, so I thought there might be something wrong with the system disk. I checked it out and created a file there to run a simple program. Somehow that overloaded the disk so that when I printed it out, some of the files crashed together and I started to get all kinds of strange stuff."

"Like what?" Bolan asked.

Reed shrugged. "Like all these dates and cities. Labeled 'Delivery Dates.' And distribution maps and coordinates. All kinds of crazy stuff like that."

"Record shipments maybe?"

"I don't see how. The store's not that big. Besides, the point of shipment was in Miami."

A heavy branch whomped the roof of the car as they drove deeper into the brush.

"Can you remember where in Miami?" Bolan asked. "An address or something?"

Ahead the road widened and the tiny cabin built by Shawnee's parents stood in a small clearing amidst the lush plants. Birds, unafraid of the intruders, cawed loudly, almost belligerently.

"An address, Dodge," Bolan repeated. "Can you remember?"

"Sure, I remember. I saw it often enough on the printer."

Bolan nodded. They were finally getting somewhere. They didn't know what the KGB was up to, but now they knew where.

Miami.

"But I swear," Reed continued, "I didn't embezzle a cent. I was just doing homework."

"Based on what you just said," Lynn explained, "I don't see how they'd ever convict you in a court of law."

Bolan snorted. "He wasn't supposed to live long enough for it to get to court."

Reed shifted uneasily in his seat, rubbing his wrists where the cuffs used to be.

Bolan pulled the Toyota right next to Belinda's parked Honda. He jumped out, helped ease Lynn out of the back seat and followed Shawnee to the front door. Rita accompanied Reed, who tagged after Bolan.

Shawnee pushed the front door open and entered. "Hey, Belinda, what the hell kind of greeting is this?"

Then she stopped dead. The others bunched up behind her. Bolan edged around her into the single room.

"Welcome," the man with the shotgun said. "Is that better?"

He was standing in the middle of the room. On each side of him stood three more men, all armed. Behind them, Belinda was tied and gagged, dark bruises splotching her face. Blood dripped from one ear.

"Clip Demoines," Shawnee gasped.

"Bingo!" Demoines grinned. "Now come on in here so I can get a good look at the famous Savannah Swingsaw." His face went grim and menacing. "A final look."

17

Clip Demoines did not look like most of the Mafia bosses Bolan had come in contact with. He couldn't have been older than midthirties. His hair was a streaky blond with dark roots. Bolan had enough experience with disguises and dyes to recognize bleached hair. And Demoines didn't dress in the usual expensive but tasteless suits of other hoods. He wore a yellow knit shirt with the little alligator on the chest, pleated twill pants with a green belt and leather deck shoes without socks. A white tennis sweater was draped over his back, the arms tied around his neck. He looked like a walking ad for summer wear. Except for the Stevens shotgun in his hands.

Demoines's eyes rested on the Executioner.

"You must be the leader of this Savannah Swingsaw."

"I don't know what you're talking about," Bolan said.

"You don't?" This amused Demoines, who again displayed his perfect teeth. He looked at Lynn's wounded arm. "What happened to you?"

"I slipped skateboarding."

He nodded. "Not knocking over another of my business establishments?"

"I don't know what you mean."

Demoines looked at all of them and shook his head sadly. "Apparently you think because I'm young and dress like this, that I don't mean business. I have an MBA from Harvard and my uncle came from Sicily. Now *that* combination means business." He tossed the Stevens shotgun to one of his goons and picked up one of the Star Model PD .45s from the table. He strolled casually toward Belinda.

"You guys think you can hit my places and get away with it indefinitely? Oh, I have to admire your guts, but not your sense. Money talks, friends, and I spread enough money around to buy up all the talk in Georgia. Most of it was a waste, dead ends. Some of it led to you people. We were just pulling up to your apartment when we saw this cutie—" he tapped the barrel of the .45 against Belinda's bruised cheek "—pulling away. Some of us went inside, some of us followed her here, asked her a few questions. Stubborn little bitch, isn't she?"

"Leave her alone," Rita said, speaking in her cop's voice.

"Fine," Demoines said. "Just answer my question."

"What question?" Bolan asked.

"Where's the rest of the Swingsaw? What are their names?"

"This is it," Shawnee said. "These two guys aren't a part of it. They were in jail, you can check that out."

Demoines laughed loudly, throwing his head

back. He looked at his men and they laughed along, more out of politeness or fear than humor.

"*You* are the Savannah Swingsaw? The four of you women?" He laughed again. "You don't understand. I don't want the ladies' auxiliary. I want the real thing. Now where are the men?"

"What you see is what you get, buster," Shawnee said.

Demoines lifted the .45 to Belinda's temple and pulled the trigger. The impact of the bullet rotoring through her brain knocked her and the chair over, splashing her blood on the wooden floor. The side of her face had powder burns. Parts of her skull were embedded in the wall behind her.

Demoines smiled. "That improve anyone's memory? If not, who's next?" He looked at Bolan.

Bolan stared back, fists clenched and teeth grinding. Never had he wanted to kill someone so much. He watched the horrified expressions on the faces of the other women, the shock in Dodge Reed's face. Yet there was nothing he could do. Not now. For a moment he understood Hal Brognola's sense of rage and frustration.

But he would get Demoines. Bolan made himself that promise. Now was not the time, not with so many guns pointed at him and the others, not with the KGB plot still unresolved. Right now he would act the role of the soldier, but sooner or later Clip Demoines would know him for what he really was, the Executioner.

"You bastard!" Shawnee screamed and sprang at Demoines.

A beefy goon in a red sweatshirt grabbed Shawnee by the arm. She snapped a knee into his crotch and he doubled over. Breaking away from his grip, she continued toward Demoines.

Demoines raised his gun.

Bolan leaped at Shawnee, clamping his arms around her chest and lifting her off her feet. She struggled against him, arms and legs flailing with grief and anger.

Bolan hugged her close, pinning her arms to her sides. "Easy," he whispered. "Wait."

He could feel the fluttering of her heart where his wrist was pressed against her chest. Slowly, she calmed herself down, finally nodding to him to release her. He did.

Her breathing was still ragged as she glared at Demoines, but she didn't move.

"See what I mean?" Demoines said. "You can't expect me to believe that women are the Savannah Swingsaw. Look how emotional you got just because I killed one of your friends. If it wasn't for the big guy there, I'd have had to kill you, too."

Demoines stepped over the splayed legs of Belinda. Her short blond hair was sticky with blood.

"Now, I'll ask again. Where is the rest of your group? Who do you work for? Another syndicate? The Gallano brothers from Memphis?"

"She told you the truth," Bolan said, keeping his voice flat and toneless. "This is the Swingsaw. They just broke me and my buddy out of jail. Check it out."

Demoines smiled. "I don't know why, but people

never take me seriously. Even though I went to Harvard. When my parents got killed in a car crash, I got sent to my Uncle Dom. He was younger than Dad, hipper. Wanted me to learn the new ways, but not forget the old ones, the ones that got us the money and power in the first place. So he sends me off to Harvard for my MBA." He stepped up to Bolan, his face solemn. "Maybe that's why you aren't taking me serious."

"Oh, I take you serious," Bolan said. "Dead serious."

Demoines smiled. "Yeah? Well, we'll see." He nodded at one of his men, the one whom Shawnee had kneed. Without hesitation the man opened the closet door. Inside, Bolan could see boxes of ammunition, the black outfits complete with hoods, axes, a couple of chain saws. The goon lifted one of the chain saws up and handed it to Demoines.

The Executioner looked at the pile of guns, the bike pack with grenades that had been taken away from them when they'd entered the cabin. Too far away; too many guns pointed at them.

"We told you what you want to know," Bolan said. "Using that won't get you anything more."

"No? We'll see. Hell, even if you're right, I'll have the fun of doing to you guys what you've done to my places. That's a good advertisement to keep anyone else from trying the same thing, wouldn't you agree?"

Demoines gripped the saw's front handlebar, flipped the toggle switch and pulled the cord. The motor's growl filled the small cabin room. He wrapped his other hand around the rear handle-grip and pressed the trigger. The cutter links hummed as they sped around the long flat guide bar. Demoines waved the buzzing saw in Bolan's face, hovering near the ears.

"Just a little off the sides, friend?" he said, chuckling. "A trim?"

Bolan didn't move. His icy gaze was fixed on Demoines's eyes as if they were alone in that room.

"Nah," Demoines said, pulling the saw away from Bolan. "I have a feeling I could cut off just about anything and you wouldn't talk. Maybe with one exception. I'll get to you later. Right now, let's start with someone else." He looked over the group, examining each as if he was judging a beauty contest. He waved the churning saw in each of their faces, but none flinched. Lynn yawned. "Tough broads," he said. Then he looked at Dodge Reed.

Bolan knew Reed wasn't up to this. The kid had held up pretty well so far, considering all he'd been through. But the murder of Belinda had put him in a state of shock. Now with Demoines waving that chain saw in his face, there was no telling what would happen.

"I'd advise you not to move," Demoines said, "not even an inch."

Dodge Reed, his pale face slicked with sweat, his eyes wide with fear, stood bolt straight as Demoines inched the whining saw closer and closer to him. Reed wasn't even breathing, afraid that would cause him to move.

Demoines teased the trigger, starting the cutters

grinding, then stopping, grinding, stopping. He eased the saw closer until the cutters were resting lightly against Reed's chest.

"Got anything to say, son?"

The young man looked helplessly to Bolan. "Tell him! Please!"

"I did, kid. He just wants to have his sick fun."

Demoines smiled at Reed. "He's right, you know. This is fun." And he squeezed the trigger. The saw whizzed to life, chewing up the front of Reed's prison shirt, just barely nicking the skin enough to draw blood. Then Demoines released the trigger.

"Leave the kid alone, Demoines," the Executioner growled.

Bolan had to admire Reed. Tears were streaming down his cheeks, yet he stood his ground. Others might have fainted, dropped to their knees to beg. Even terrified, he managed to hold himself together. But Bolan realized that wouldn't be good enough. Next time, Demoines would shove that saw straight into Reed's chest.

"Gutsy kid," Demoines said, ignoring Bolan's words. "Let's see what the loudmouth big guy is made of."

He turned away from Reed, smiling, but there was no humor in his face. It was hate. He pressed the trigger and started the saw whirring as he walked slowly toward Bolan, the saw aimed at Bolan's chest.

One of the nearby goons took a step back as if he was afraid of being splashed with blood.

Everyone was staring at the churning cutters, mesmerized by their nasty sound and motion.

Bolan didn't move.

Demoines was grinning now, his black Sicilian eyes gleaming under the crop of bleached blond hair. He was less than two feet from Bolan's heart.

The Executioner exploded into action.

While everyone was staring at the blade, Bolan spun out of the way, leaping at the nearest Mafia soldier. Bolan seized his wrist and shoved the startled man directly at Demoines. It all happened too fast for Demoines or the goon to react.

But not the saw.

The thug's hand slammed right into the cutters in a splatter of blood and bone. The saw hummed hungrily, chomping through the wrist until the gunhand dropped to the floor with a thud, the weapon skittering to within a few feet of Bolan.

The wounded man held up his handless wrist, blood making darker stains on his red sweatshirt. He ran toward the other goons, holding up his stump as if pleading for help. Taken by surprise they dodged him, as if afraid what he had might be catching. He crashed wildly into one hardguy, knocking him over.

Demoines was so startled he dropped the saw.

A couple of his men regained their composure enough to aim their guns in Bolan's direction.

But the Executioner was moving again.

He dived to the floor and scooped up the dropped gun, then rolled onto his side and firing upward. His first two shots dropped two henchmen.

"Kill them!" Demoines bellowed, running for cover of the sofa near the fireplace. "Kill them all!"

But it wasn't that easy. Shawnee, Rita and Lynn

were also moving now, scavenging the dead bodies for weapons, returning fire. Dodge Reed managed to get one of the guns and began blasting away, never coming close to hitting anyone, but making enough noise to help scatter the Mafia scum.

"Out!" Bolan commanded, yanking open the front door and waving the others through.

One of Demoines's men popped up from behind a highback recliner and fired at Bolan, missing him by inches. Shawnee stopped, went into her double-grip stance and blew the side of his face off from scalp to ear. Panic and adrenaline caused her to fire two more shots into the already dead body.

"Come on, Shawnee!" Bolan urged her.

She took a deep breath, turned and dashed through the door. Rita St. Clair and Lynn Booker followed. Only Bolan and Reed remained. Bolan ran back into the room, picked up the two S&W .357s and stuffed them into his pants. Then he swung the bike pack of grenades over his shoulder, and yanked Dodge by the elbow, hauling him through the door toward the car.

"Start it," Bolan said, tossing the keys to Shawnee.

She jumped behind the wheel as the others piled into the car.

A mobster stuck his head out the door and began firing a pump-action shotgun. The rear side window of the car blew out. Bolan squeezed off a round from the S&W .357, which caught the punk just below the elbow, smashing his arm. The man screamed, his arm dropping uselessly to his side, the gun tumbling to the dirt.

A cabin window shattered as gun barrels popped out to take aim. The Executioner fired a couple of rounds through the window and the gunmen ducked out of sight. He heard Demoines's rabid voice desperately yelling to attack.

"Mack!" Shawnee called. She swung the car around, braking it in front of Bolan and flinging the passenger door open. "Let's go, mister. This party's getting boring."

Bolan dived into the front seat as a volley of slugs tattooed the Toyota's doors and fenders. Shawnee gunned the engine and the car kicked up dirt as it tore down the road. A tree along the narrow road bumped the door closed behind Bolan.

"I didn't see their cars," Bolan said.

"They must've parked them farther down the main road, then walked to the cabin. This is the only way in."

"Good, they won't be following us too soon."

"But they will follow us," Shawnee said.

Bolan nodded. "Yeah, they'll be coming. No matter where we go."

"Where *are* we going?" Dodge Reed asked. He was breathing heavy from the adrenaline, but his eyes were clear.

"We're going to the point of origin of those shipments you discovered in that computer. We've got to find out exactly what it is they're shipping that they'd kill to protect."

Shawnee glanced at Bolan. "Miami?"

"Miami," Bolan repeated.

Everyone was silent as they bounced along the bumpy dirt road. Most of them were thinking about

Belinda, mourning her loss. Bolan understood this and didn't disturb the silence. What he had to say next could wait a few more miles.

18

Clip Demoines sat behind his desk and picked at the green alligator on the chest of his blue shirt. His feet, sockless and clad in deck shoes, were propped on top of his huge mahogany desk. The desk had been his uncle's, the very one he'd been sitting at the night Clip had shot him in the back.

Things were arranged downtown and burglary was claimed. Someone was even arrested for the crime, though he was mysteriously stabbed to death in prison before he came to trial. Books were closed on Uncle Dominick's unfortunate demise.

"I want them, Tom," Demoines said calmly into the telephone. He listened patiently, then interrupted his friend. "I don't have time for the excuses and bitching today. This one's important. You get the usual amount plus a $50,000 bonus. Agreed?" Demoines listened. "I don't care what excuse you use, Tom. You're the cop, think of something cop-like. I gave you the car make and model and the license number. Now you find them. Today." He hung up.

Clip Demoines leaned forward, ran his fingertips lightly along the smooth varnished wood. That made him feel better. The only flaw in the wood was a tiny chip where Uncle Dom's front tooth gouged out a nick when, after Clip had shot him, his head had fallen onto the desk. Demoines had left the little flaw in the wood unfixed. For sentimental reasons.

A loud knock at the door.

"Come on," Demoines said.

The door opened and Ron Thaxton entered. Thaxton was Demoines's lieutenant and adviser. It had been his advice that Demoines not go personally to see the Savannah Swingsaw last night. He had suggested sending an army of men to wipe them out while he and Demoines were seen at some social function. But Demoines had wanted to be there, to personally punish the scum who had busted up his places, who had cost him money.

For Demoines could stand anything but the loss of money. That was personal, as if someone had raped him. For that there was only the ultimate punishment. Death.

"So?" he asked Thaxton.

Thaxton shrugged. "Word's out all over the state. Everybody's on the lookout for the car and they've got the descriptions of all the people."

"Especially that big guy. The one in black. I want him, Ron, you understand that?"

Thaxton nodded. He understood that there would be no other business until this matter was settled. That despite his Harvard MBA, Clip Demoines was still a hood at heart. He still believed in vendettas and all that stuff. Sometimes such things were good business, but there was a time, Thaxton thought, when it was best to cut your losses and run. You didn't need a goddamn MBA to know that much.

Demoines rose and began pacing behind his desk. "That man, the big one, I want to know everything about him you can dig up. Check the fingerprints we lifted, check his story about jail. Check everything."

"I will, Clip."

"You'd better, Ron," Demoines said, stopping to face his lieutenant. "Because by tomorrow night he's a dead man. Or you are."

THOUGH THE VOICE ON THE PHONE was solemn, there was a faint hint of glee, as if he was secretly pleased at Zavlin's failure.

"I will have to make a full report, Gamesman."

Zavlin smiled into the phone. "Of course."

"Detailing your failure."

Zavlin winced. There it was again. That word—failure. Control had managed to work it into the conversation three times now. It was not a word he'd had occasion to hear before in regard to his own work. He did not want to ever hear it again. "Have you alerted our people?"

"Yes." The control sighed, as if to say it was a hopeless gesture. "Every road, every town, every bus station, train depot, plane terminal to Miami is being watched. Seems a vast expenditure of manpower, a waste of time."

"We must assume that the boy Reed told this Damon Blue what he saw in the computer."

"But it is doubtful that the boy knew what any of that meant."

"Doubtful, yes, but not impossible. Besides, whatever he knew or didn't know, he's undoubtedly told Mr. Blue by now."

"But this Damon Blue is nothing more than a petty crook, a thief."

Zavlin chuckled hoarsely. "Perhaps. But not likely."

"His records say—"

"Never mind his records. I saw him in action. I saw the way he moved, the way he handled himself. This man is no petty crook. He is much, much more."

There was a thoughtful pause. When the voice spoke again, it was hesitant, a little frightened. "Now what, Gamesman? You know the importance of the mission. What we are doing now will erode the entire economic structure of the United States, possibly plunge them into the worst depression in history."

"I know the stakes, Control," Zavlin snapped. "Our aim now is to locate and kill them before they leave the state. We don't want any violence to take place near the distribution warehouse. That might cause undue interest in our activities."

"Yes. Yes, that is true."

Zavlin grinned. Control was nervous, quite willing to relinquish all responsibility into Zavlin's capable hands. "All we must do now is wait for our contacts to report. Our network of paid informers is second to none. Once they are spotted, I will go there and kill them."

"Indeed," Control said, gathering some of his courage again. "We can afford no more failures."

That word again, Zavlin grimaced and hung up. He brushed a hand through his white hair. He would make the man in black pay with more than his life for allowing the word *failure* to be spoken in the same breath as the name of Zavlin.

19

"Forget it!" Rita St. Clair said. "I'm not doing it!"

Lynn Booker, holding her wounded arm, agreed. "Neither am I. It's stupid."

"It's not stupid," Bolan said patiently. "It's good sense. They're going to be on the lookout for us all through this state and Florida. Look at us. Traveling together we're not too hard to spot."

Rita shook her head. "Okay, then we split up and meet in Miami."

"No. You travel separately, each in a different direction. Except south. That's where they'll be looking for you."

They were parked by the side of the road with a map of Georgia spread out on the hood. The car was a blue Nova they'd hotwired and driven off a used-car lot a couple of hours before. They'd switched plates at a roadside diner.

Shawnee looked up from the map at the two women. "Mack's right," she said sadly. "We have to split up for now. Rita can go up and visit her folks."

"Swell," Rita said bleakly.

"Lynn, you take off for San Francisco. Get lost in the Asian community."

The Oriental nodded.

"Let's get moving," Shawnee said, "we've got some plane tickets to buy. At different terminals, of course."

Rita, Lynn and Dodge Reed climbed back into the car. Bolan folded the map and looked at Shawnee. "Thanks for helping me convince them. I can do this better alone," he said.

Shawnee lowered her voice. "Like hell. You don't think I believed that crap, Mack? Sure, I think they should get to safety, but I'm still going with you."

"Uh-uh!" Bolan said.

"They won't be looking for a couple. It'll be a cinch to sneak by them."

"You don't believe that?"

She shrugged. "Maybe not, but I'm going along anyway."

Bolan realized there was no point in arguing. She would do what she wanted and short of knocking her out, he couldn't stop her. Part of him was pleased.

"What about me?" Dodge Reed asked as Bolan pulled the car back onto the highway.

Bolan patted the folded paper in his pocket. "Is this page everything you can remember from the computer?"

"Yeah, I wrote it all down."

"You positive this is the right address?"

Reed hesitated. "I think so."

"Okay," Bolan said. "You better pick a state with a friendly climate, because that's where you're going until this is all over."

"I've got a girl in Atlanta. Can I at least call her,

tell her I'm going? Ask her to get my class assignments?''

Bolan laughed harshly. "I wouldn't, Dodge. For the next few days anyway, school is definitely out.''

THE CAR HISSED AND STEAMED, smoke snorting from the seams of the hood.

"Damn, what now?" Shawnee said, pulling over to the side of the road.

Bolan woke from his light nap, his eyes immediately wide awake. "Trouble?"

Shawnee gave him a disgusted look. "Just the kind of trouble you'd expect from a car stolen from Sam Friendly's Used Car Lot.''

Bolan looked at the odometer. She'd taken them another 127 miles. This state seemed endless. But Bolan knew they were close to the Florida border, just outside of Waycross, near the Okefenokee swamplands. Down the road a quarter mile from their steaming car was a sign announcing the nearby Okefenokee National Wildlife Refuge and Wilderness Area.

Bolan popped the hood and jumped back to let the steam spray into the air.

"How bad is it?" Shawnee asked.

"Can't tell yet."

"Looks like a hose."

Bolan fanned away some of the steam and leaned over the engine. There was a rip in one of the ancient radiator hoses. Bolan loosened the clamp to examine the hose.

"Not too bad," Shawnee observed. "Fixable."

"Got a knife?"

Shawnee shook her head. She patted her pockets and pulled out a fingernail clipper. "Will this do?"

Bolan frowned. "It'll have to." He sawed the split end of the hose off and refastened the clamp. It would hold. But he was more disturbed by what else he discovered. Sam Friendly hadn't exactly gone all out on fixing up this used car. The wires were frayed and loose, the engine gritty, the hoses cracking. "Problems," he said.

"What?"

"Looks like this engine's been driven through the swamp a few times."

"Maybe a 'shiner's."

"Moonshiner's?"

"Yeah. They don't make the stuff much anymore, but they do their share of hauling booze and cigarettes up north without the tax stamps on it. Make a lot of money."

Bolan pointed to a wire leading from the distributor cap. "The steam from the busted hose finished off what was already a pretty sad spark-plug wire. It'll run, but we've got to get it to a service station."

"We passed Patterson a few miles back."

"What's ahead?"

Shawnee shrugged. "Blackshear, then Way-cross."

"Okay, let's drive into Blackshear, get this fixed, then get the hell out of there."

"What if we're spotted?"

Bolan gave her a hard look. "It's a chance we'll have to take. No other choice."

Twenty minutes later they rolled into Blackshear. Bolan spotted a service station with a phone booth at the paved entrance. He told Shawnee to look for a mechanic as he slipped out of the car.

Bolan stood next to the pay phone and played with the coin-return button. As soon as the phone rang he snatched it up. "Yeah?"

"Can't a guy even go to the damn john without getting beeped?" Brognola's voice was gruff, but Bolan could hear the relief in it. "So, I guess you're still alive."

"Most of us." He explained what had happened.

"That's it?" Brognola asked, when Bolan finished speaking. "All this over some dumpy address in Miami?"

"Apparently."

"How do you want to proceed?"

"Well, right now I have to assume both Zavlin and Demoines are after us, so we're trying to sneak past them into Florida."

"Maybe I should just send a squad to that address and arrest everyone there."

Bolan thought about it. "I don't think so. We can't be certain that what we need to know is there until we investigate. But even more important, can you guarantee no security leak to the KGB from your end?"

Brognola hesitated. When he answered his voice was low. "No, I can't."

"Then let Shawnee and me poke around first, see what we can find out. I'll call you afterward."

"I could meet you there." There it was again, that hopeful tone, ready for action.

"I've never seen anyone so anxious to get shot at."

Brognola chuckled. "Things aren't the same without Stony Man Farm. I feel a million miles away from the action now."

"Sometimes I wish I could say the same."

Brognola snorted, not buying that. "Okay, guy, get back to the business of saving the world, huh?"

"Sure, pal, as soon as the mechanic over there finishes working on the car."

"Then what?"

"Then we drive in to Waycross, which is a big enough town that I can switch cars."

"Okay. Keep in touch."

"Sure thing," Bolan said as he hung up.

Shawnee was just coming out of the rest room as he walked over to the service station.

"Can your phone pal help us?"

"Not much. Not yet."

She shrugged. "Doesn't matter. We can handle it."

"Like your attitude."

Bolan walked over to the mechanic, who was just returning to the Nova after stopping to pump gas into a dusty pickup truck. "How much longer?"

"Not much," the mechanic said. It was hard to determine his age because of the grease on his face, but Bolan figured him to be around fifty. He was stick-thin and chewed tobacco, occasionally pausing to spit some brown juice into the dirt.

"Time enough for us to grab a bite?"

The mechanic looked up at Bolan and Shawnee, then back into the engine. "Suit yourself."

Shawnee took an angry step toward the man. "Listen here, buster," she said, her drawl becoming more pronounced the deeper into the South they drove. "We gotta get to my daddy's funeral over in Needmore in two hours. My mama needs us there to help out. Now me and Tucker here been on the road all day and we just...." Tears started to puddle in her eyes. "We just *gotta* make it in time to see daddy once more."

The mechanic stopped chewing his tobacco, looked Shawnee over. "Thirty minutes, gal. Meantime you can catch a bite down the street at Rhonda's Café. Food ain't good, but it's hot and cheap."

Bolan placed a comforting arm around Shawnee and led her away. "Thanks," he said to the mechanic. Shawnee sobbed quietly, glanced up, winked and returned to her sobbing.

In the café she ordered vegetable soup and corn bread. Then she ate part of Bolan's chicken-fried steak, mopping up his gravy with her corn bread.

"Help yourself," Bolan teased, spreading the map out on the counter. "Any suggestions?"

"We could take 23 down to Jacksonville. Or 84 to 441 and cross over near the Suwannee River."

"Pretty public either way. What about here?"

She shook her head adamantly. "No way. We don't want to even go near the Okefenokee. Anything east of Jones Creek or west of Toms Creek is swamp, infested with 'gators. We get caught in there we'd be better off dropping in on Clip Demoines and handing him a new chain saw."

"Okay. We'll go through Jacksonville, try to get lost in the traffic."

They paid, left a tip and went back to the service station. The mechanic was adding a quart of oil to a station wagon. Bolan checked the engine, paid him and he and Shawnee drove away.

They were still a few miles from Waycross when Bolan spotted the dusty pickup truck in his rearview mirror. "Get the guns out," he calmly told Shawnee.

She reached under the seat, dislodged the two S&W .357s and placed them both in her lap. She didn't look around. "You sure?"

"He's been following us since the service station. Same beat-up truck that stopped for gas there."

"Aren't many good roads around here. Maybe he's just going in the same direction."

"Maybe." Bolan nodded. "But he slows down when I do and speeds up when I do. And those rifles in his rack probably aren't for show."

"What's he waiting for?"

"I suspect for whoever he called ahead to. My guess is there's a car or truck full of armed good ole boys on their way toward us right now."

Shawnee sighed. "Ain't we ever going to be alone without bullets nipping at our butts?"

"Maybe. But not this time." He swerved the car onto the side of the road, purposely churning up a thick cloud of dust behind him. He spotted a side road about half a mile ahead. "Any idea where that leads?"

"Nope. But we're pretty close to swampland."

Bolan pointed to the Jeep speeding down the highway toward them. Rifles started to appear in the three passengers' hands. They were aiming.

Shots clapped and the hood was pockmarked with two holes. Steam seeped up through one of the holes.

"Great!" Bolan said, wheeling the car onto the dirt road. The pickup and Jeep were right behind him, the dust obscuring their vision enough to throw their shots off.

Bolan stomped on the gas pedal and the Nova rocketed down the road, bouncing from side to side. He didn't know where the road was going, except that it was away from the men with guns.

He and Shawnee didn't try to return fire. The way the car was rocking, shooting would be a waste of ammunition.

"I don't like the way that engine sounds, Mack," Shawnee said, referring to the clanking and pinging. More steam rose from the bullet holes in the hood.

But the car still had life, and Bolan squeezed it for all it was worth, whipping around curves and urging the screaming engine even faster.

A sign on a wooden gate ordered all vehicles to stop and turn around, dangerous marshlands ahead.

"Hell," Shawnee said, as they busted through the gate, sending splintered wood somersaulting. "This is the goddamned Okefenokee Swamp, Mack."

"So it is," he said, racing down the road, the pickup and Jeep still close behind. A couple of miles later, the road gave out to grass, then mud. By the time they reached the first sandy ridge, the car sputtered and died.

Gunfire hailed down on them as they rolled out of the car and into the grassy marsh.

Bolan ignored the warm sticky water seeping into his shoes and through his pants. He returned fire at the pickup, watching the windshield shatter. He saw the driver grab his face, and ducked as the pickup truck swung wildly to the left, hit the sandy ridge and rolled over onto its roof, crushing whatever was left of the driver.

The Jeep stopped a little farther back. The three armed men hopped out and dropped to the ground. Then the driver turned the Jeep around and headed back up the road.

The Executioner guessed they were returning to contact Demoines. If these were Zavlin's men, they would have contacted him first, not sent a jeepload of gunmen.

The three men fired sporadically, not enough to threaten Bolan and Shawnee, but enough to keep them pinned down until Demoines and more men arrived.

"What now?" Shawnee asked. "Never mind, I think I know."

Bolan nodded grimly. The two of them bellied into the dank water and silently waded deeper into the swamp.

20

"How many gunners do we have?" Demoines asked, thumbing a shell into his Weatherby Regency double-barreled shotgun. "I'm talking guys who know how to shoot, not cracker assholes with .22s."

Thaxton checked his list. "We've got three guys out there right now, keeping them warm for you. They've all grown up around here, so they know the area and they know how to hunt. One's an auxiliary cop in Waycross."

Demoines snorted. "Big deal." He tugged the bill of his green safari hat. "Who else we got?"

"It's short notice, Clip."

"I didn't ask for the time, Ron. I want a goddamn report."

Thaxton took a deep breath. "I got three of our regular boys, shooters from Atlanta. But I've got to warn you, they don't know much about stumping through swamps."

"For what I'm paying them, they'll learn."

"Yes, boss."

"Okay," Demoines said, "adding everybody together, we've got eight fully armed men with shotguns and rifles against a man and a woman with handguns."

"Don't you think that's a bit of an overkill?"

Demoines frowned. "You didn't see them fight. Especially that big guy." He clenched his teeth in anger at the memory.

A thump sounded on the door of the Waycross hotel room where they were staying. Thaxton opened it a crack, conferred, then turned to Demoines. "They're ready."

Demoines walked over to Thaxton. He spoke slowly, tapping his shotgun on Thaxton's chest with every word. "I want them, Ron. Real bad."

"MORE COFFEE, SIR?" the pretty waitress asked.

"A little more, please."

The young woman leaned over to pour the beverage, her tongue lodged in the corner of her mouth with concentration. But as she strained in her uncomfortable position, her hand shook, and she spilled coffee into the saucer, some of the dark liquid splashing on the chipped Formica table.

"Oh, my," she said. "I'm terribly sorry."

Zavlin yanked some napkins from the dispenser and mopped up the coffee from the table. "Quite all right." He wanted her to go, but she became flustered, standing there apologizing, glancing over her shoulder to see if her boss was looking.

"...first week and all. But I'm getting better. Hardly ever spill any. I don't know why...."

Zavlin looked out the window, saw Demoines and his hunting party climb into the Jeep.

"...just nerves, I guess, from working for my cousin. He's a sweet guy, but he...."

Zavlin turned to the young waitress. "Leave me," he snapped.

She looked startled, almost tearful, but she left.

Zavlin stared back out the window. Five in the Jeep. Plus the three he'd heard about. Eight. He hadn't heard how many they were hunting, but he hoped one of them was Dodge Reed. That would save him the trouble of killing the kid himself. Secretly, he admitted to himself that he hoped the big man in black was not among the ones that were trapped out there. No, he wanted that man for himself. He patted his traveling bag, felt the weight of the branding iron packed in among the shirts, pants, shoes and toiletries. The running iron he hoped to be able to use on that man someday.

He looked at the clock above the smoking grill. It had been only a couple of hours since KGB informants had told him of the violence Damon Blue and the others had had at a remote cabin with Mafia chief Clip Demoines. He knew Demoines would never rest until he'd chased down the man who'd humiliated him. So he'd kept a tag on him, following him to Waycross.

Zavlin was familiar with the Mafia boss, since the KGB did extensive business with the Mafia. The dossier on Demoines suggested a certain emotional imbalance, a desire to be accepted by polite society yet still maintain control over his underworld empire. The result was a ruthless, quick-tempered man. Not to be underestimated.

But then, neither was the big man in black. He'd escaped Zavlin's assassins as well as Demoines's thugs. Whoever he was, Zavlin wanted him. Patience, Zavlin told himself. Let the Americans splash about in the bug-infested swamp. Meantime, he would wait and see what would happen with Demoines's hunting party.

Zavlin plucked the menu from behind the ketchup bottle. Suddenly he was quite hungry.

21

Shawnee plucked a clump of smelly swamp grass from her hair. "Jeez, Mack, you really know where to take a girl for a good time."

"Makes you almost miss Saigon, huh?"

"Almost."

They were on their knees in the shallow water, the sucking peat mud molding around their legs. Mosquitoes buzzed them like fighter squadrons. Bolan and Shawnee swatted at them, crouching low in the water, but kept their guns dry.

"They haven't moved," Shawnee said.

"They won't until Demoines shows up with reinforcements."

She looked around her at the dense lushness, swatted another mosquito. "Shouldn't we be getting away before they arrive?"

Bolan grinned. "Get away? To where?"

"It's not the 'to where' that I'm worried about. It's the 'from what.' From Demoines and his goons." She pointed at a green sign sticking up through the swamp. "See that? It marks the canoe path. We follow it and we're bound to run into some people we can hitch a ride with. Or even find one of the tour boats the park service runs through here. Demoines wouldn't shoot us in front of them."

"Probably not. But the park officials are going to ask some tough questions about what we're doing here. Remember, lady, I'm still wanted as both Damon Blue and Mack Bolan."

"Well, we can't sit in the mud all day waiting for them to come after us. I've been on the tour before, Mack. They got more than twenty-thousand 'gators in this swamp."

Bolan looked at her and smiled. "At least there aren't any sharks."

"Ow!" She swatted a fat mosquito on her arm, smearing the skin with the blood it had just sucked. "I wouldn't be too sure of that, Mack."

He peered up through the trees. "It'll be dark soon."

"Is that supposed to cheer me up?"

"Relax," he said. "Enjoy nature."

She slapped a mosquito on her neck. "Nature is overrated." She leaned closer to him. "I'm serious, Mack, what are we waiting for? Okay, so we avoid the tour boats and the canoes and we just wade past the snakes and 'gators and stuff and come out somewhere else."

"On foot?"

"At least we'd be alive."

"But maybe too late to get to that Miami warehouse in time."

She shook her head in exasperation. "You're impossible."

"Listen, Shawnee. Our car's dead, but Demoines

will be back in that Jeep. While they're out tracking us, we sneak back and steal the Jeep. That leaves them on foot and gives us a little extra headstart. Simple.''

"Except for the fact that they'll be shooting at us.''

He wiped the mud from her cheek and kissed the clean spot. "Nothing's perfect.''

They waited in silence, Bolan keeping an eye on the three men with rifles. The men still fired a round or two every few minutes, but since they had no idea where Bolan and Shawnee were now, the shots were more habit than threat.

Bolan looked around, studying the swamp. Kneeling in the slimy water was like being in the mouth of some salivating monster.

There was a desperation about the swamp, as if it knew it was one of the last outposts in the world of primitive beauty. But even here there were signs of encroachment. The canoe trail signs. A floating gum wrapper.

And now Demoines and his men.

The Jeep bounced down the rough road, past the smashed wooden gate. Men were jumping out before the Jeep even stopped moving. They were running toward the swamp, guns ready. Demoines walked slowly, brashly, as if savoring what he already knew would be a sweet victory.

Demoines walked to the edge of the road, took a dainty step into the mushy swamp and sank up to his knees in water. The other men joined him immediately. "Hey, Blue!" Demoines yelled. "I know who you are now. Why don't you save everybody a lot of trouble and come on outta there?''

Bolan didn't answer.

"What's the point, Blue?" Demoines continued. "Eight of us are gonna comb through this shit until we find you. The longer I gotta stand in this crap, the more pain it's gonna cost you and your lady friend. Come out now, you both get it quick, and easy. Over and done."

Shawnee snorted. "Generous cuss, ain't he?"

Bolan pulled her down farther and whispered into her ear. "You follow along that sandy ridge until you're behind them. When they're far enough away from the Jeep, you start it up and get the hell out of here."

"What about you?"

"I'll lead them away from the Jeep."

"Yeah, but what then? How do you get out? I'm not leaving without you."

"You won't be," Bolan said.

Demoines's voice rose again. "You're wasting time, Blue."

A flock of birds cawed and flapped their wings in response.

Bolan continued his instructions to Shawnee. "Once you've driven out of sight, they aren't going to bother chasing you on foot. They'll keep coming after me. I'll sneak around, come up behind them right where our Nova is, and you come burning rubber and pick me up."

"How do I know when to come back?"

"Give me ten minutes from the time you take off. Understand?"

"How do I start the thing?"

"Don't worry, they probably left the key in. They wouldn't take the chance of someone carrying it out here, getting shot and floating off with the key. But if there isn't one, just keep running. Okay?"

Shawnee nodded.

"Go." He gave her a gentle nudge.

And she was gone.

Bolan watched her wade through the swamp, keeping out of sight behind the cypress trees. When she was safely on her way, he went to work.

The Executioner knew he had to keep Demoines and his men from spreading out and accidentally discovering Shawnee. That meant telling them where he was. Loud and clear.

He stood up behind a giant tupelo tree, brushed aside a thick clump of Spanish moss and watched Demoines detailing his goons into some kind of flanking movement. Bolan smiled, lifted his .357, steadied the eight-inch barrel against a branch and fired.

A man in a red plaid shirt was jerked back off his feet, rifle flying up into the air. He flopped backward into the water and never moved again.

"There!" Demoines pointed, teeth bared. "There he is! Kill him!"

The seven survivors opened fire at once, chipping hunks of wood from the tupelo, ruffling the lacy Spanish moss but not being able to get a clear shot at Bolan. Who was already moving deeper into the swamp.

They stopped firing and ran after him, occasionally slipping in the muddy peat, tripping on a submerged tree root.

Bolan used the thick underbrush to keep them from getting a clear shot at him. Sporadic gunfire broke the marshy stillness, and bullets whizzed by much closer than he liked.

A hazy dimness hung over the swamp as twilight hit the outside world. Visibility would be even worse now, but Bolan knew how to use that to his advantage.

They were resting now, waiting for Demoines to stop wheezing and catch his breath. The Mafia boss handed his Weatherby shotgun to one of his men while he leaned over and retched into the swamp. His men turned their heads.

Bolan smiled and ran even deeper into the swamp, his splashing footsteps taunting them.

Up ahead a young man in a park-service uniform was poling a flatbottomed johnboat toward Bolan.

"Hey, fella," the young man called out sternly. "This here ain't hunting season, you know. Let me see your permit."

Bolan spun around and pointed the .357 into the young man's face. "Out!" he commanded.

The young man stuck his pole back in the boat and jumped into the water. He tried to speak, but nothing coherent came out of his mouth.

"I don't have much time, son," Bolan said slowly, "but you'd better listen carefully. There's a pack of men coming this way with rifles and a desire to kill anything human they see. I figure your best bet is to get lost as fast as you can."

"Y-y-yes, sir."

"Good boy. Now get going."

The young man, with hands still held over his head, ran through the water with remarkable speed. By the time Demoines got here, they might hear the distant splashes, but they wouldn't see him clearly enough to shoot.

Bolan silently climbed into the flatbottomed johnboat. It was only about twelve feet long and five feet wide, made of aluminum and painted camouflage green. There was no motor, just the pole that was forked at one end to keep it from sinking into the peat. Bolan had been in something similar once called an alligator punt, a boat pointed at both ends made from cypress boards. That's where he'd first used a pole to propel a boat.

Slowly, silently, he muscled the pole into the mud and guided the boat across the water.

"What's that?" he heard someone shout, thinking they meant him, but relieved when he heard the panicked reply.

"'Gator!"

A volley of shots churned water.

"Stop it!" Demoines snarled. "That's a log, not an alligator."

Just then the Jeep engine rumbled to life.

"The Jeep!" Demoines hollered.

Bolan stopped the boat behind a thick tree and watched them scramble toward shore. They started firing, but the jeep was already roaring off into the distance. That gave him ten minutes to get by Demoines and his men.

Bolan slipped over the side of the boat, pushed it out in the direction of his pursuers. They were still too far away to see it, but in another twenty yards they would. However, it would be too dark for them to determine if he was in it or not.

Bolan grabbed the forked pole and waded away from the drifting boat.

"Forget her!" Demoines said, stopping the shooting. "She's gone. But she was alone, I'm sure of that. That means Blue is still here. He's the one I want." He raised his voice. "You hear that, Blue. Your little honey took off on you. Left you for dead meat. Guess she was smarter than you thought, eh?"

Bolan submerged himself until only his head and right hand clutching the gun were above the slimy water. He crawled on his knees now, edging past them, only fifty yards to their left, while they marched straight ahead.

"Come on, fan out," Demoines ordered. "You two go that way. Tanner, move to the left. It's getting dark and I don't want him to slip by us."

Bolan stopped as he watched the hefty man named Tanner splash toward him. Fortunately the gunman was moving sideways, keeping his eyes out front like the rest of them. Still, Bolan couldn't afford to move, to make any noise. Tanner kept coming closer. Bolan had no choice but to duck underwater, head, gun and everything.

He waited, holding his breath, squeezing his eyes closed. The water felt greasy swirling around his face. Still he heard Tanner's boots splashing closer.

Not knowing how close Tanner was, Bolan didn't

want to risk attracting attention by moving, even underwater. But his lungs were starting to burn, his throat convulsing for air. He fought the urge to break surface.

"There!" Tanner yelled excitedly, pointing out at the flatbottomed johnboat.

Bolan took advantage of the distraction to lift his head out of the water, just as Tanner opened fire at the vessel.

"A boat," someone else said.

Now Demoines was opening fire and then everyone was.

Tanner stood firing only eight feet away from Bolan. Amidst the din of shooting, Bolan began crawling away toward the shore where Shawnee would return any minute now.

The movement caught Tanner's eye. Bolan saw him swing his rifle around, eyes wide with discovery, struggling to warn the others and shoot at the same time.

Bolan didn't give him a chance. Fearful that the swamp water might have affected the .357, Bolan just lunged at Tanner with the forked pole. Tanner took the fork directly in his chest. The sharp wooden prongs punched through the chest like a stapler and Tanner dropped into the water unheard by the others, who were running toward the boat, still shooting rifles and shotguns.

Bolan wedged the pole sticking out of Tanner's chest under a rock, keeping Tanner hidden under the water. Then he continued toward shore.

It had been ten minutes, maybe more, by the time

he reached the sandy ridge near the Nova. Where was Shawnee?

"It's a goddamn boat, all right," Demoines was shouting at his men, "but where the hell is Blue?"

"Maybe we hit him and he sank under the water," one man suggested.

"Then find his body. I want to see the blasted body."

"Hey, where's Tanner?" another goon asked.

They all began to look around, calling Tanner's name.

There was a long tense silence. Then Demoines shouted hysterically. "Go back! Back to shore. He's circled behind us."

And now they were all charging toward Bolan, shouldering their rifles and firing.

Still no sign of Shawnee.

Bolan dashed for the Nova, pulled open the front door and grabbed the bike pack of grenades that Belinda had packed for him. He plucked one out, yanked the pin and tossed it into the swamp.

One man screamed as the water boiled in front of him, the hot twisted shards of metal scraping off his face as they spun by him.

Honking horn. Growling engine.

Shawnee skidded up to Bolan.

He dived over the Jeep's door into the back seat, holding onto the roll bar as Shawnee whirled the Jeep around and gunned it out of there. Demoines's team fired at the fleeing vehicle, but no slugs scored.

Bolan tossed the bike pack of grenades next to his

feet and stretched his long legs out into a comfortable position. He closed his eyes. "Wake me when we reach Miami."

ZAVLIN LIFTED HIS EYES from the *Wall Street Journal* and watched the parade of muddy men stomping through the hotel lobby. He recognized Demoines's clothing before he recognized the dirt-encrusted face.

"Give me the damn key," Demoines ordered the desk clerk. "I lost mine."

The desk clerk immediately complied, offering to send up a bellboy to gather the clothes and have them cleaned and returned by morning.

Demoines ignored him and marched to the elevator.

Zavlin smiled. He counted men. Fewer.

He studied Demoines's angry face. Loser.

So, the man in black had won again. No matter, Zavlin thought, folding his paper. If the man was an agent working for the government, Zavlin's sources would have identified him as such by now. Or the government would have already raided the warehouse. Neither had happened, so it was safe to assume this man was a loner. Working on his own. Perhaps a mercenary who hoped to blackmail the KGB.

Of course, as a loner he wouldn't even know that the KGB was involved, just that something illegal was going on. Good. Zavlin could deal with greed, but patriotism was something else, much more difficult to suppress.

Zavlin tucked the newspaper under his arm and strolled through the lobby toward the door and a taxi to the airport. There could be but one place for the man in black to go now. Miami.

And Zavlin intended to be there first. Waiting.

22

The sign on the chain-link fence read Seaway Chemical Corporation.

Bolan stooped under the sign and began snipping the metal strands with wire cutters.

There were still a good two or three hours of darkness left. Plenty of time to take a quick look around.

From the outside the warehouse was just as dark as all the other warehouses in this industrial district. The difference was that while the parking lots of the other buildings along the street were empty, this one had more than a dozen cars.

Security guards patrolled the perimeter, so Bolan had to work fast. Despite the patches on their shirts that said Protectall Security Services, Bolan had a hunch they were KGB-trained. That meant they would kill on sight.

He severed the final link, peeled back the fence and wriggled through. He jumped quickly to his feet and ran, then pressed himself against the wall, until he was hidden in the deep shadows.

The windows were all painted black so no one would know they were running a late shift here. Perhaps during the day Seaway Chemical Corporation was a legitimate business, filling the usual orders as part of its cover. But at night, its second shift was up to something. Something the KGB wanted to cover up by killing a hapless college kid.

And the only way Bolan would uncover this secret was to penetrate the building.

That hadn't been his intention. He'd told Shawnee it was just a little scouting run, to get a feel for the layout. She'd insisted on coming along, but he'd managed to talk her out of it for once. He'd given her Hal Brognola's phone number and told her to call him if she didn't see Bolan back at the motel in an hour. He still had plenty of time.

His wounds ached a bit, undoubtedly from his high jinks in the swamp. As soon as they'd reached the motel, Shawnee had washed and redressed the wounds. Then she'd gone out and bought them both new clothes while Bolan had stayed in the room cleaning his S&W .357.

Now he was here. Miami. The address Dodge Reed had witnessed on that record-store computer screen the night he'd tried to sneak in and do his homework. After coming this far, Bolan had to know what it was all about.

A side door opened and the bright light from inside flooded over him. He scooted back along the wall, melding into the shadows.

A man stepped out into the night air and stretched his arms and back. He was wearing a white surgical mask and cap, a long white lab jacket and disposable rubber gloves. He pulled the gloves off and threw them in a large cardboard barrel near the door. Then he pulled down his mask, let it droop around his neck and lit a cigarette. He took a deep drag, let out a long satisfying sigh and leaned against the wall.

The door opened again, light bloomed and a woman stepped out. She peeled off her gloves, tossed them into the barrel, removed her mask and took a puff from his cigarette while she fumbled in her lab jacket for her own pack. They were both in their early thirties.

"Damn heat," she said. "I can hardly breathe in there. Especially with these dumb masks."

He shrugged. "It's a bitch. But it's better than getting any of that stuff in your lungs. You see what happened to Tulley last week when he took his mask off to scratch his nose."

She nodded. "No great loss. He was a lech."

"Yeah, but he worked fast."

"Ha! Nobody works fast enough in there. They got Superbrain screaming at us all the time. 'Do this. Do that.' Shit, he may be some kind of genius or something, but he sure is a pain in the ass."

The man nodded in agreement.

"Well," she continued, "at least we've made the deadline. The first shipment went out today. The rest tomorrow morning."

"Bonus time." He grinned.

"And I know just how I'm gonna spend mine. Club Med in Playa Blanca. Lots of sun and gorgeous hunks."

He laughed, stubbed out his cigarette. "Gotta get back. Already got a lecture about the evils of smoking from Superbrain."

"See ya, Stew."

"Right." He went inside.

She lingered another minute, puffing on her cigarette.

Bolan would have preferred the man to stay. At least then the lab jacket would have fit.

FIVE MINUTES LATER the Executioner entered the door with the woman's mask tied over his nose and mouth. Her hat had been extra large to accommodate her long hair, which she wore piled in a bun under the cap. It was still a little small for Bolan, but not as small as the damned lab coat. He pulled it on, rolling up the sleeves and not even trying to button it. He hoped they would think he was merely on his way to the rest room or something. Besides, he didn't intend to be there very long.

Immediately inside the door was a roll of disposable gloves. He squeezed his fingers into a pair and wandered down the corridor into the main plant area.

People in similar outfits worked diligently, controlling huge vats, giant mixers, machines of all sizes and varieties. At the end of the production line a green powder was funneled into big cardboard barrels.

The labels on the barrels showed a cluster of oversize vegetables and fruits surrounding the product's name: Eden-Plus. A chemical formula was printed beneath it.

"Certainly you cannot see clearly from here?" the voice behind Bolan said in a friendly tone.

Bolan spun around. The man wore a surgical mask too, but Bolan could see the one blue eye and the one brown eye. And in his hand, a 9mm Tokarev.

"PHOTOSYNTHESIS," Zavlin said.

"Plants," Bolan said. "That's the process they use to convert sunlight and water into oxygen."

"More or less," Zavlin said.

"More," Subrov said. "So much more."

They were sitting in one of the offices away from the main production area. A filter system cleaned and recirculated the air in the room to allow them to remove their masks.

Bolan sat in a chair against the wall. Zavlin ran one hand through his white hair and used the other to hold his gun leveled at Bolan's chest.

Subrov was in his early twenties, with gaunt cheeks and hollow eyes. He had a certain intensity that indicated obsession.

"Dr. Subrov is only twenty-one," Zavlin explained with some annoyance, "but he is in charge of this project."

"Exactly what is this project?" Bolan asked.

"No need for you to know, Mr. Blue. If that is your real name. I will ask you several questions. You will answer them without hesitation."

"And if I hesitate?"

"I will kill you."

"And if I speak?"

Zavlin smiled. "I will kill you, of course. But there is death and there is *death*. One is much more uncomfortable."

"I've been hearing that distinction a lot lately."

Zavlin raised an eyebrow. "I suspect that is because you are the type of man who leaves his enemies no other choice."

"What's all this got to do with plants?" Bolan asked.

"It is not your concern," Zavlin repeated firmly. He was a professional all the way. There would be no bragging or explanations. Just interrogation and then death.

But his young comrade was not so experienced. He was pleased to have yet another ear to explain his own brilliance. "It was my idea," Subrov said, pointing his bony finger at Bolan. He leaned up against the blackboard next to his desk. There was chalk dust in his black hair and some on his pants.

So this is Superbrain, Bolan thought.

"I discovered the process while in the university at Moscow when I was fourteen. But it took me another seven years to perfect." He was lecturing now, as if addressing a classroom of admirers. "How, I asked myself, could the proper nutrition be introduced into the masses who are basically resistant to anything healthy? How do we combat their stubborn ignorance and the stupidity of the individual for the greater good of the whole?"

"Likes people, huh?" Bolan said to Zavlin.

Zavlin's jaw was clenched. Bolan could sense the man bristling. Apparently this hundred-and-twenty-pound kid carried more weight with Moscow than even the great Zavlin.

"Photosynthesis, that's the key," Subrov continued. His accent was British, with only a hint of Russian in the vowels. "If we could interrupt the photosynthetic process by which a plant produces carbohydrates...." He picked up a piece of chalk and attacked the blackboard, writing a complex chemical formula. "Then we are using the glucose units as they link together to form starch as pockets to hold these nutrients. If we also consider that in the light reaction, the energy of an absorbed photon of light is used during the enzyme-catalyzed transfer of an electron from an unknown molecule to a carrier—"

"Which all boils down to what?" Bolan said.

"Boils down?" Subrov said, annoyed at the interruption. "Ah yes, you mean what is the end result?" He dropped the chalk on his desk and stared contemptuously at Bolan. "You are a very rude man."

Bolan waited. He knew the kid's arrogance would force him to tell, to show off to one more person.

"It 'boils down' to this. We can now introduce certain substances into plants, merely by sprinkling the substance onto the leaves. Eventually, the plant absorbs it, transforms it until it becomes a part of the plant itself. Simple enough?"

Bolan nodded. "You're saying that if you sprinkled nutrients on a tomato plant, that plant would add the nutrients to the tomato. The person eating the tomato would be healthier."

"Yes. Something like that."

"But somehow I have a feeling you aren't shipping nutrients around this country."

Subrov hesitated. "Nutrients were only one aspect of my discovery. There are other chemicals that can also be introduced."

"Like what?"

The Russian youth smiled. His sunken face and oversize teeth made his head look a little like a skull. "Like synthetic heroin. Also a substance I created. We sell it as pesticides to your farmers. They spray their crops. The synthetic heroin is absorbed and reformed as part of the vegetables and fruit you eat. The physical reactions will not be immediate. They take years to develop, and even then only in certain body types.

"But then those who are affected will have all the symptoms of heroin addiction. The excruciating pain, the epileptic fits. The physical and psychological damage will only be the start. Our scientists and economists estimate that the reduction in productivity by these people will cause staggering economic collapse. Not to mention the panic and mass hysteria of the rest of the country as they try to discover what this affliction is. But by then, of course, it will already be too late."

Bolan's face was stone, the features chipped from some blazing comet. The eyes glared with anger. "From nutrients to help the masses to mass poisoning. Some leap for a genius."

Subrov shrugged. "I do what is right for my country. And for science. What does your country matter anyway? Beach Boys and jeans, that is all they know."

"Enough," Zavlin said. "You have had your say,

Dr. Subrov. And you too, Mr. Blue. Now it is my turn.''

He walked over to the laboratory table where test tubes and flasks and chemicals were set up. There, leaning on a metal stand, directly over the blue flame of the gas Bunsen burner, was a branding iron. The tip of the iron glowed a fearsome red.

Zavlin slipped a leather glove on his right hand, transferring his gun to his left hand. He picked up the handle of the iron and carried it carefully toward Bolan.

The boy genius watched with a detached curiosity, as if interested only in how flesh might react when introduced to a glowing iron.

Bolan sat rigidly in his chair, not moving.

"You may scream, Mr. Blue," Zavlin said, coming closer. "But movement might be fatal. Any attempt to knock this away and I will have to shoot you."

And suddenly he pressed the tip of the running iron against Bolan's thigh. The pants hissed and smoked as the iron burned through and sizzled against the skin. Bolan flinched, his hands gripping the side of the chair as if to crush it. But he made no sound.

Zavlin pulled the iron away and smiled. "That was just a touch. Nothing like what will happen next. Are you ready to speak?"

Bolan said nothing. There was no point. The truth would only make things worse. They'd kill him immediately. As long as they thought he was holding out, they'd keep him alive.

"I have work to do," Subrov said with a bored expression. "Please clean up when you are finished." He started out of the office, but was stopped by a uniformed guard wearing a surgical mask. He was dragging Shawnee beside him. She wore no mask, so her curses were very clear.

"Bastard!" she spit, punching and kicking at the guard. One kick caught him in the shin and he angrily threw her against the wall.

"What's going on?" Zavlin demanded.

"She was sneaking through the fence," the guard explained. "They'd used wire cutters."

"I'm so sorry," Shawnee said to Bolan. "I couldn't wait. I had to help you." She saw the burn on his thigh. Her eyes widened with horror, then anger. "What have they done?" She fell to her knees to examine the wound.

"Tie her to that chair," Zavlin told the guard. Then he smiled at Bolan. "Let's see if she is as indifferent to my branding iron as you are."

The security guard grabbed Shawnee by the arm, yanked her to her feet, then threw her into the chair next to Bolan's. He reached to his holster for his cuffs.

But when his hand came up, it was gripping an S&W .38. And the guard was spinning around, pointing the gun at Zavlin.

"Move it, Mack!" Hal Brognola said to Bolan as he tugged his mask down.

Zavlin was caught by surprise, but his reflexes were astounding. He jumped to the side just as Brognola fired. The shot gouged a hunk out of the blackboard. Zavlin fired back, the Tokarev kicking 9mm Tokagypt cartridges around the room. One sliced across Shawnee's hip, drawing a little blood but doing no major damage.

Dr. Subrov, the twenty-one-year-old Superbrain, ran blindly for the door, saw Brognola with his big .38, spun and ran directly into Zavlin's scorching iron, impaling himself on the sharp tip. The hot metal seared through cloth and flesh, between ribs, and finally through the heart, boiling blood as it sank deeper into his chest.

Zavlin released the iron and fired at Brognola. The big Fed dropped behind the desk and prepared to fire back, but Bolan had leaped across the room and had his hands around the KGB assassin's throat.

One of Zavlin's security guards burst into the room spraying bullets, but Brognola cut him down with two rounds to the face.

Bolan had his hand around Zavlin's wrist and was banging it against the floor, trying to shake the gun free. Finally the hand opened and the gun flew out.

And then the Executioner went to work.

He didn't need to think about the van of cons or guards that Zavlin had had killed, or the other past victims of this assassin. He didn't even have to think of the hideous plot they'd been hatching right here, the attempt to addict innocent people.

He didn't have to think of all that, but it helped. Helped him gather the strength as he dug his elbow into Zavlin's throat, crushing the windpipe. Then hammered blow after blow into the Russian's face, smashing every bone. Or when he twisted the head until the neck crackled like a little boy's stick being dragged across a picket fence.

23

"That's it. Room 27." The man pointed a dirty fingernail across the street at the motel.

Clip Demoines gave the man five hundred dollars.

The man looked at the bills for a moment, then whined, "But you said a thousand, Mr. Demoines."

Demoines glowered at the man and he scurried off into the night.

"Okay, Ron," Demoines said to Thaxton. "One more chance to redeem yourself. Only this time, let's do it right." He popped open the trunk of his Mercedes and pulled out two 9mm semiautomatic Uzis. He handed one to Thaxton.

They each slammed in a 25-round magazine, snapped in the folding stocks and thumbed the safeties off.

"Ready?" Demoines asked.

Thaxton hesitatated.

"What's wrong now?" Demoines said.

"This is Gianguzzi territory, Clip. We're not supposed to hit anybody down here without getting permission."

"Fuck Gianguzzi. I hit who I want, where I want.

And right now—'' he glanced across the street at
Room 27 ''—I want that guy dead. And his bitch,
too.''

Thaxton looked across the street. The door to
Room 27 opened and the big man came out. He was
shirtless and barefoot, carrying a cardboard ice
bucket.

''We could drop him right now,'' Thaxton said.
''No one will see us in the dark.''

''No,'' Demoines said. ''I want them both. And I
want them to see me pulling the trigger.''

Thaxton sighed. ''Okay, Clip.''

Bolan returned to the room, knocked on the
door. Shawnee opened it, wearing only a shirt. Her
long sinewy legs reflected the flashing red neon
Vacancy. She giggled, blocking the door with her
body. He wrapped an arm around her waist and
carried her inside. The door closed.

Demoines's upper lip crawled with sweat. ''I
hope they're doing it when we bust in. I really hope
so.''

They climbed back into the Mercedes, Thaxton
behind the wheel. Sunrise was less than an hour
away. They crossed the deserted street, pulled up to
the curb and left the motor running as they got out.
No one was around.

''What about neighbors as witnesses?''

Thaxton shook his head. ''None on either side.
Hardly anybody in the whole place. I guess that's
why they picked it.''

But Demoines wasn't listening anymore. He was
smiling, his finger twitching anxiously on the trig-

ger. Thaxton was at his side now with an Uzi in his hands.

They reached the platform at the top of the stairs. Demoines kicked the door in and began peppering the bed before he even realized there was no one in it. He jerked his head at Thaxton, who ran into the bathroom, tearing the shower curtain open but finding no one.

"The closet," Demoines said. Together they stalked toward the closet, guns aimed, standing slightly aside in case the man and woman were armed.

The Mob boss gripped the knob and slowly turned. He eased the door open. It caught for a moment, stuck. He pulled harder. He heard a click, but the door opened the rest of the way. He and Thaxton jumped in with both guns pointing.

The closet was empty.

Except for a string of green Christmas bulbs strung across the closet, each dangling from a wire hanger. And the string that ran from the bulbs to the inside door handle. Only they weren't Christmas bulbs at all, Demoines noticed.

They were grenades!

Thaxton must have realized that a second before Demoines, for he turned to run for the door. But too late.

The grenades exploded in a whoosh of heat and whirling metal that pulverized the top halves of their bodies, grating them down to tiny strips of mushy flesh.

24

From behind the motel, Bolan, Shawnee and Brognola watched the explosion illuminate what was left of darkness with bright angry lights.

"Wouldn't it have been simpler to shoot them?" Shawnee asked.

"Simpler," the Executioner said. "But not as just."

"You know, Mack, I used to think I knew all about you. Now I'm thinking that I'm only just starting to understand what makes you tick."

Brognola handed Shawnee his jacket and gestured at her bare legs. "You might get cold."

"Thanks. Squeezing through motel bathroom windows in the middle of the night can give a girl a reputation."

Bolan watched the smoke billowing straight up into the sky. He felt good. Tired, but good. As if he'd cleansed not just some evil part of the world, but some dead part of himself. Shawnee had helped him see that.

"I'm sorry about your friend Lyle," Brognola said to Shawnee. After the battle at the warehouse, he'd told them both about what Zavlin had done. Shawnee had gone off by herself a few minutes.

When she'd returned, her eyes were red and watery.

Bolan had looked at Zavlin's body and wished he could kill him again. But then he'd thought of Belinda Hoyt and decided to do the next best thing. He'd made a few calls and put the word out where Clip Demoines might find a certain escaped convict named Damon Blue.

And they'd waited.

Demoines's private jet didn't keep them waiting long.

Now Belinda and Lyle could both rest a little easier.

The three of them listened to the sirens of the approaching fire engines.

"What now, Shawnee?" Brognola asked.

"Same old stuff. Regroup the Savannah Swingsaw."

"But Demoines is dead."

"They'll just send somebody else. As long as there's profit, the Mob will be there. The trick is to take away the profit. That's what the Swingsaw intends to do."

"Or take away the Mob," Bolan said.

"That's not our way, Mack. That's another thing I learned being with you. As hard as I try, I can't be like you. So I've got to do what's right for me."

Bolan wrapped an arm around her shoulder and hugged her tight.

"But you'll be hearing from us," she said to both men. "Just read your newspapers. You'll be reading about the Savannah Swingsaw again."

Brognola groaned. "I was afraid of that. Just as

long as it's not in the same article as Mack Bolan. That combination is enough to make the South rise again.''

"Stranger things have happened," Shawnee said, smiling.

Brognola started walking away. "I guess you kids don't need me around anymore. Have to get back to Washington before they notice I'm gone and move my desk out into the hallway.''

Bolan watched his friend stroll across the parking lot, a spring in his step. He heard whistling. Bolan called after him. "I guess that desk will be a lot easier to handle after tonight.''

"For a while," he answered. "For a while.''

They headed for the car Brognola had rented for them. Inside was an envelope with five thousand dollars and a note. "Take a vacation. And please, don't tell me where.''

Bolan started up the car.

"Where are we going?" Shawnee asked.

"I don't know yet. You mind?''

"No. I kind of like it.''

They pulled out into the street, heading west.

"You know, Mack, there's always room for you with us.''

"Us?''

"Savannah Swingsaw.''

He smiled. "As leader?''

"No way," she bristled, then laughed. "Coleader. You and me.''

Bolan remembered Stony Man Farm, Able Team, Phoenix Force. The dream gone bad.

"I don't play team sports any longer."

She nodded, scooted closer to him. "Then how about some one-on-one?"

Bolan reached over and patted her knee. She'd forgotten to give Hal his jacket back. The thought of settling down with Shawnee was tempting. She was tough and self-reliant, with a way of looking at right and wrong he admired. But it wasn't to be. Not yet anyway.

For now, they were heading west in a legal car with five thousand dollars in cash and nobody in particular hunting them. And that would have to do.

For now.

MORE ADVENTURE NEXT MONTH WITH

MACK BOLAN

#75 The Bone Yard

There's a wild card in Vegas.

The Mafia, the Japanese Yakuza and the
Vegas Old Guard each want control of the city.

Mack Bolan is the new player and he's dealing in death,
with skills learned in a hell called Nam and honed to a
sharp edge in the urban jungle.

To shave the odds the Executioner pulls a Joker from the
deck, Tommy Anders. The game is down to one last
hand—winner take all.

Available soon wherever paperbacks are sold.

DON PENDLETON'S EXECUTIONER
MACK BOLAN

Sergeant Mercy in Nam.. The Executioner in the Mafia Wars... Colonel John Phoenix in the Terrorist Wars.... Now Mack Bolan fights his loneliest war! You've never read writing like this before. By fire and maneuver, Bolan will rack up hell in a world shock-tilted by terror. He wages unsanctioned war—everywhere!

GOLD EAGLE

Available wherever paperbacks are sold.

Mack Bolan's

ABLE TEAM

by Dick Stivers

Action writhes in the reader's own street as Able Team's Carl "Mr. Ironman" Lyons, Pol Blancanales and Gadgets Schwarz make triple trouble in blazing war. To these superspecialists, justice is as sharp as a knife. Join the guys who began it all—Dick Stivers's Able Team!

"This guy has a fertile mind and a great eye for detail. Dick Stivers is brilliant!"

—Don Pendleton

#1 Tower of Terror	#9 Kill School
#2 The Hostaged Island	#10 Royal Flush
#3 Texas Showdown	#11 Five Rings of Fire
#4 Amazon Slaughter	#12 Deathbites
#5 Cairo Countdown	#13 Scorched Earth
#6 Warlord of Azatlan	#14 Into the Maze
#7 Justice by Fire	#15 They Came to Kill
#8 Army of Devils	#16 Rain of Doom

Able Team titles are available wherever paperbacks are sold.

GOLD EAGLE

Mack Bolan's
PHOENIX FORCE
by Gar Wilson

Schooled in guerrilla warfare, equipped with all the latest lethal hardware, Phoenix Force battles the powers of darkness in an endless crusade for freedom, justice and the rights of the individual. Follow the adventures of one of the legends of the genre. Phoenix Force is the free world's foreign legion!

"Gar Wilson is excellent! Raw action attacks the reader on every page."

—*Don Pendleton*

Phoenix Force titles are available wherever paperbacks are sold.

GOLD EAGLE

GET THE
NEW WAR BOOK
AND MACK BOLAN
BUMPER STICKER <u>FREE!</u>

Mail this coupon today!

FREE! <u>THE NEW WAR BOOK</u> AND
MACK BOLAN BUMPER STICKER
when you join our home subscription plan.

Gold Eagle Reader Service, a division of Worldwide Library
In U.S.A.: 2504 W. Southern Avenue, Tempe, Arizona 85282
In Canada: P.O. Box 2800, Postal Station A, 5170 Yonge Street, Willowdale, Ont. M2N 6J3

YES, rush me <u>The New War Book</u> and Mack Bolan bumper sticker FREE, and, under separate cover, my first six Gold Eagle novels. These first six books are mine to examine free for 10 days. If I am not entirely satisfied with these books, I will return them within 10 days and owe nothing. If I decide to keep these novels, I will pay just $1.95 per book (total $11.70). I will then receive the six Gold Eagle novels every other month, and will be billed the same low price of $11.70 per shipment. I understand that each shipment will contain two Mack Bolan novels, and one each from the Able Team, Phoenix Force, SOBs and Track libraries. There are no shipping and handling or any other hidden charges. I may cancel this arrangement at any time, and <u>The New War Book</u> and bumper sticker are mine to keep as gifts, even if I do not buy any additional books.

IMPORTANT BONUS: If I continue to be an active subscriber to Gold Eagle Reader Service, you will send me FREE, with every shipment, the AUTOMAG newsletter as a FREE BONUS!

Name	(please print)	
Address		Apt. No.
City	State/Province	Zip/Postal Code
Signature	(If under 18, parent or guardian must sign.)	

This offer limited to one order per household. We reserve the right to exercise discretion in granting membership. If price changes are necessary you will be notified.

116-BPM-PAE5

AA-SUB-1R

Mack Bolan is a Winner!

Readers everywhere applaud his success.

"You deserve some kind of reward for delivering such reading pleasure to millions of people throughout the world."

M.L.,* Chicago, Illinois

"Bolan isn't a killer—he is a positive force fighting the degeneration of man. He is also awesomely entertaining, as fine a literary hero as any."

S.S., Augsburg, Germany

"I want to congratulate you on your decision to put our Sergeant into the fight against terrorism. With the world situation today, it will endear many more people to this man of courage."

B.C., New York, New York

"I am in the army, and I would be proud to serve with Mack Bolan and cover his back down the first mile, and second, and third if he said it was needed."

P.E.D., APO, New York

"I think my Executioner collection is the finest thing I own, or probably ever will own."

R.C., Gainesville, Florida

*Names available on request.